FATHERS AND
FUGITIVES

ALSO BY

S.J. NAUDÉ

The Alphabet of Birds
The Third Reel
Mad Honey

S.J. Naudé

FATHERS AND FUGITIVES

*Translated from the Afrikaans
by Michiel Heyns*

Europa
editions

Europa Editions
8 Blackstock Mews
London N4 2BT
www.europaeditions.co.uk

This book is a work of fiction. Any references to historical events,
real people, or real locales are used fictitiously.

Copyright © 2023 by S.J. Naudé
First publication 2024 by Europa Editions

Translation by Michiel Heyns
Original title: *Van vaders en vlugtelinge*
Translation copyright © 2023 by Michiel Heyns

All rights reserved, including the right of reproduction
in whole or in part in any form.

The extract from "Trees" in *The Complete Poems of Philip Larkin* by Philip Larkin
is reproduced with the kind permission of Faber & Faber.

A catalogue record for this title is available from the British Library
ISBN 978-1-78770-543-2

Naudé, S.J.
Fathers and Fugitives

Cover design and illustration by Ginevra Rapisardi

Prepress by Grafica Punto Print – Rome

Printed and bound in Great Britain by Clays Ltd, Elcograf S.p.A

CONTENTS

1. WHERE THE WOLVES MATE - 13

2. LOST IN MALAYSIA - 59

3. HANKAI - 91

4. THE BIRTH PAINS OF TERMITES - 153

5. THE CITY OF FATHERS AND SONS - 199

ABOUT THE AUTHOR - 217

For my brother

FATHERS AND FUGITIVES

1. Where the Wolves Mate

The scale of the painting is modest. Still, Daniel is captivated by the horizontal streaks of washed-out colour—or, rather, the light shimmering through the practically non-existent pigment.

Behind him, a man's voice booms: "It's enough to send me to sleep!"

When Daniel looks round, the man feigns a yawn. Gold fillings glimmer in the molars. "See," the yawner says to his companion, pointing at Daniel. "It's irritating him too. Nobody's fooled." He waves away the other rooms. "We've seen the whole lot. It's all the same painting. Hundreds of them. Like photocopies." Then he waggles his index finger between himself and his friend. "Not like us. We're full of big colours, I tell you!"

Daniel tries to place the accent. Slavic. Both men are now looking at him—the tall one with his compelling glare, his loose-limbed companion with the ironic mouth. The painting is the last one in the exhibition, but the first one Daniel is seeing. To avoid the crush, he always starts at the end—the crowd has thinned by this point.

Daniel's first impulse is to smile tightly and move on, but he stays. The two keep gazing at him, exchanging a few muttered sentences in an Eastern European language. The tall one switches to English—breathlessly, as if a life is at stake. "Don't you also find it boring?" Once again he vaguely gestures at the rest of the exhibition. The hollow at the base of his throat throbs. A few chest hairs emerge from his T-shirt, moving in sync with the pulse. He breathes, sounding calmer now. "Rather come and have coffee with us?"

It's a Tate Modern retrospective of Agnes Martin, the American minimalist. For weeks Daniel has looked forward to—and postponed—coming. The exhibition is ending today, and the museum is closing in an hour. He's a fervent admirer of Martin's series with their barely discernible variations. Of the colours and dimensions that change every few years by just a shade or a centimetre. Of the silence, the drifting and dispersal. Daniel casts a quick glance down the exhibition rooms multiplying like echoes in the distance, each as brilliantly lit as the one before. From here, indeed, the serried paintings seem undifferentiated. Daniel looks at the man, at the glittering fillings in his dark mouth, smiles wryly. "Okay then. Coffee."

The two are sitting opposite Daniel in the cafeteria. Serbs, it transpires. It is late winter. All three of them, seated against a glass wall, keep their overcoats on. Outside, beyond the glass, all is blue and bleak. Their reflections are brighter than their corporeal selves—their scintillating twin brothers are sitting out there in the cold. Unshivering, as if nothing is amiss.

The quieter one presses his knee against Daniel's. He gazes frankly at Daniel while his companion talks incessantly, with urgency. Diverse topics surface, which he addresses briefly, feverishly, and then abandons for a fresh one. Daniel doesn't say much, only divulges, when questioned, that he lives partly in London and partly in Cape Town. Why, the talker demands. Daniel reflects for a moment. He shrugs, dismisses the question with a wave of his hand. "A long story. I thought I was swopping one continent for another. Now it feels as if my true home is on aeroplanes, in the frozen skies over Africa..."

Oliver is the name of the talkative one. His laconic companion is Yugo. It doesn't take Oliver long to tell their story. The two of them quit Serbia. They're in London to start a new life. "Life will be paradise here!" Oliver exclaims, wide-eyed. Again and again Oliver emphasises what a homophobic place Serbia is. How careful they had to be there, how furtive their lives. He recounts instances of violence, a gang of youths who flung them to the ground and kicked their skulls. "We had to flee, believe me," he says. "There was no choice!" Otherwise they could've had a good life there, Oliver explains. He was a film reviewer for a Serbian paper and also hosted a movie slot on a television programme. "We sacrificed *everything* for our freedom." His hands open out as if he's dropping something, letting it break.

Yugo's expression is pained. "Everything," he echoes.

"And we are happy to befriend as many people as possible." Oliver extends his hand firmly, as if meeting Daniel for the first time. Daniel proffers his own hand gingerly. Oliver shakes it with vigour, for several seconds.

"Pleased to meet you," Yugo contributes, regarding Daniel from under his eyebrows. His knee nudges Daniel's ever more insistently under the table.

For a while they're silent. Then all three look to the outside at once, at the echo table, at their hardier, colder brethren. Rain is now dribbling down the glass, distorting the faces looking back at them. A waiter presents the bill. Without anybody saying a word, Daniel pays and the three of them get to their feet.

They follow the river eastward, their heads in a cloud of breath. The Serbs make small talk: British weather, where they're staying, what they like about London. The conversation now feels more constrained than back in the museum. Occasionally Oliver exchanges a few words in Serbian with Yugo.

At London Bridge they take the steps up from the riverbank. By now Daniel knows that the two of them are renting a room in Archway, that they could take the Northern Line back from here.

"Come and have a glass of wine at my place," Daniel says impulsively. Oliver and Yugo exchange brief glances, nod. They head south down Borough High Street.

When they enter the flat, Daniel flips shut the laptop on the dining-room table.

"This place is beautiful. Really beautiful," Daniel hears Oliver's voice from the main bedroom.

Yugo goes to the bathroom, locks the door. Daniel picks up Yugo's coat from the sofa, hangs it up.

"I have to go and buy cigarettes," Oliver says, returning to the living room. Daniel hasn't seen him smoke, and he doesn't smell of it. They've also just walked past several shops selling cigarettes.

"Go ahead," Daniel says hesitantly. "Just press the intercom when you get back."

For a while, Daniel sits on his own in the living room. Yugo emerges from the bathroom, sits down next to him, on the edge of the sofa. He places a hand on Daniel's knee. "May I?" he asks, grinning. It's not unexpected, but it is sooner than expected. His boldness disarms Daniel, relaxes him somewhat. Yugo takes off Daniel's shirt. It's a cold day and the heating is turned down too low. Daniel shivers. Then Yugo takes off Daniel's trousers and his underpants. He proceeds systematically, purposefully. He remains fully dressed himself. Daniel watches Yugo's head burrowing into his lap. He feels dissociated, as if it's the head of an actor in a play. He looks up at the ceiling, closes his eyes. After a minute he inhales a huge gulp of cold air. Yugo swallows, sits up and wipes his mouth. He smiles and dresses Daniel again, with equal meticulousness.

Oliver returns. He has not bought cigarettes, but beer. Half a dozen cheap cans. The kind that soccer hooligans drink litres of before beating the shit out of each other outside pubs, leaving the streets slick with blood and urine.

"For a while," says Oliver, not evidently apropos of anything, "we had a room with a single bed. Imagine that, Daniel—a single bed! At night I was a security guard. By day Yugo was a waiter. We saw each other only in the morning and the evening in the shower. Scrubbed each other's backs, then crawled into sheets still warm from each other's bodies."

Oliver's face now looks like a bloodhound's. His head lolls forward. He's sitting on the edge of the sofa, could slide off at any moment and land on the hard floor with a hiccup.

"Wine," he says.

"Wine?" Daniel asks. "Can I bring you some?"

"No." Oliver shakes his head vigorously. "I don't want anything. But I was just thinking. You said: 'Come to my place for wine.' But nobody has drunk any wine."

Daniel gets up. "I'll pour you a glass right away. I have a bottle in the fridge."

"No!" The vehemence in Oliver's voice stops Daniel in his tracks. Yugo places a hand on Oliver's leg, utters a single word in Serbian. Then Oliver mumbles, more demurely: "No, thanks. I'm okay."

"I'm sorry, Oliver. I was under the impression that you preferred beer."

Oliver's head keeps lolling. Yugo looks askance at Daniel.

"You know what you notice as a waiter in London?" he asks suddenly, loud and bright. He waits for Daniel, standing in the centre of the room, to guess.

"No, Yugo, I don't know," says Daniel, conciliatory. "Tell me."

"Not a single restaurant in this city rinses its lettuce. Everybody in London—*everybody*—eats snails with their salad."

Two days later, Yugo phones. He and Oliver are inviting Daniel to see an opera. "Can you buy us tickets, friend Daniel?" Like Oliver, he talks loudly, but he's better natured and less anxious, his voice always on the edge of laughter.

They meet in the foyer of the English National Opera. It's an insipid contemporary American opera. Afterwards they go to a wine bar in Covent Garden.

"Wasn't that a work of genius!"

It takes Daniel a moment to figure out that Oliver is referring to the opera. He's not sure if he's being ironic or sincerely airing an opinion.

"I found it pretty ordinary," Daniel says. "Good production values couldn't salvage the music or rewrite the libretto."

Oliver regards him expressionlessly. Then his narrative veers abruptly to a time when he was working at Starbucks. He recounts the tactics of people who don't really come to buy coffee, who for instance just pour themselves a little cardboard jug of milk, or collect handfuls of sugar sachets. Or who in the chaos of rush hour make off with someone else's coffee from the collection counter.

"One woman did it daily. So I ran after her one day. When I grabbed her by the shoulder, she was shit scared. But I shook her hand, told her, 'Congratulations! I admire you!' She never came back."

Daniel turns to Yugo. "What did you do in Belgrade?"

"Worked for a humanitarian organisation," he replies. "After the war." Daniel keeps looking at him, at the laughter lines around his eyes, but Yugo doesn't elaborate.

"You know what?" Oliver asks. "That television slot I had, the one about new movies. That was cancelled before we left! Not many people in Serbia care about art films. And they don't like to see a gay talking on TV!"

Looking through the lens of imputed Serbian prejudice, Daniel would not have guessed this solid, larger-than-life man was gay.

"I'm sorry to hear that. I'm sure it was important for you."

"What the hell, Daniel. What's important is that I can still watch movies. And that I'm making good new friends." Oliver rests a heavy hand on Daniel's shoulder, starts talking about the director Jan Švankmajer, about his work in clay and animation. Oliver is particularly fond of *Little Otik*, a film in which a childless couple adopt a tree trunk as their child.

"What do you do for a living?" Yugo interrupts.

"I'm a writer," Daniel says. "Fiction sometimes. Bits of journalism. Mainly on South African issues. The British broadsheets' tattletale from the colonies, you know."

Yugo's laughter lines crinkle. For a few moments Oliver looks at Daniel uncomprehendingly, then brightens. "Oh, but you have such a beautiful flat! You must be very successful!"

Daniel meets his friend Mirko—lecturer in architectural history at Birkbeck College, and also a Serb—for dinner. Mirko has lived in London for more than a decade. Daniel tells him about Oliver and Yugo, about their tribulations in Serbia, how he's taken them under his wing (is that what he's doing, he wonders when he hears himself utter the phrase).

As Daniel continues his account, he feels progressively more light-headed. He listens to himself as if to a stranger.

Mirko tilts his head. His scepticism is palpable. "Any educated Serb—gay men in particular—had every conceivable opportunity to flee that country long ago. I would take their account with a pinch of salt. And I would caution you."

"Against what?"

"Don't ask me." Mirko lifts his hands, declining responsibility. "All the same, be on your guard."

"Shall I introduce you to them? Then you can rely on your cultural radar, advise me?"

Mirko cradles his coffee mug in both hands. "I have no desire to make their acquaintance."

Daniel meets his two new friends at London Bridge Station. They are all warmly dressed, and they take a long walk. They drink beer in a riverside pub. Oliver is explaining why he doesn't have a Serbian name. "My mother was a hippy, she had Californian fantasies," he says, frowning. "I'm surprised she didn't name me Eagle or Storm. Or Starshine or River. Or some Apache name. He-who-hunts-wolves. Something like that." Oliver pauses, as if thinking up more names. "I saw her naked every day, my mother," he says. "Every day. Everything was permitted in our home. You know, she even saw me wanking as a teenager." He presses a hand to his groin.

Daniel doesn't know what to say. His blood pulses strongly in his temples; absent-mindedly he slips his hand under his own shirt, touches his belly. He turns to Yugo: "What about your mother?"

"Well, she's dead, isn't she? Died in the war."

I'm sorry, Daniel wants to say, I didn't know. Oliver intervenes, returns to a topic he touched on in the course of his monologues in the Tate Modern cafeteria: Sokurov films. He starts talking, breathlessly, about the unbearable intimacy between the main character and his ailing mother in the film *Mother and Son*.

"How about it, Daniel? Can we come and stay with you for a while?" Yugo blurts out unexpectedly, interrupting Oliver. "Just till we've found our feet in this big city."

For how long? Daniel wants to say. Or: But you have a room, don't you? Or: We'd have to discuss how something like that could work. But seeing the intense expressions of the two men facing him, he hears himself say: "My spare room is free. You can come."

The two look so relieved. And surprised. Daniel has surprised himself. Remarkable, he thinks, what boredom—such a sequence of empty, hardly varying days—can do to you. You'd rather introduce some variables, rather confront adventure or risk, than wander around the Tate Modern in your own cloud of silence. Or sit day after day on your own in front of a computer, your hands paralysed on the keyboard. Let what must be, be.

The presence of the Serbs in the flat is unexpectedly light. They demand little, are careful not to inconvenience Daniel. At first they spend long hours in their room with the door shut. Daniel isn't sure what they're doing. Reading, he assumes. Or perhaps they're sitting petrified, wide-eyed, covering their mouths, terrified of disturbing him. Walking past, Daniel puts an ear to the door. Nothing.

Yugo prepares the food Daniel buys and the three of them eat together. After the first week, Yugo offers to do the shopping. He chooses a downmarket supermarket, buys mainly frozen or processed foods. The next time, Daniel tries to hint subtly at better stores, at other possible purchases. When this doesn't have the desired effect, Daniel provides Yugo with a list, noting shops where he can find each item, even adding brand names. It takes Yugo hours to return, long after suppertime. He is beaming. "There are just so many interesting products and people! You could spend all day wandering among the shelves!"

A few days later Daniel sends Yugo to Borough Market, on a Friday when there are fewer tourists and Yugo will hopefully be less easily distracted. While Yugo is out among tables laden with organic vegetables and quails and wine and fish, Daniel is seated at his computer, fingers poised over the keyboard. In the last few days he's started experiencing that familiar though rare perturbation in the chest—a kind of sickness, a lovely infection. Something *must* be written. It's still a struggle, but the words do, after all, start trickling. A trickle that Oliver comes to interrupt with hands caressing Daniel's shoulders and chest. Daniel stiffens momentarily, then contracts his stomach so that Oliver can slide a hand into his jeans.

Oliver unbuttons his own shirt. "I can smell it!"

"What can you smell, Oliver?" Daniel watches Oliver throw his shirt to the floor.

"Your creative power, of course!"

What Daniel smells, is the umami fragrance and bitterness of Oliver's belly hairs against his cheek.

There is something so ordinary about their cohabitation, as if it's always been this way. Neither of the Serbs is now working; their days keep pace with Daniel's slower rhythm. The three of them go for walks, as if they've been married for years. And they watch movies. Oliver projects them onto the living-room wall with a tiny device he connects to his iPhone. Oliver is obsessed with certain directors. He waxes passionate while watching his favourite films, delivering a frenetic running commentary. He becomes frenzied. Sometimes he pulls at his hair. Once, he tugs at his own shirt so hard he tears off a few buttons. Another time he grabs Yugo by the shoulders and shakes him. The rocking Yugo looks at Daniel, smiles voluptuously. But Oliver doesn't touch Daniel—when they're both at home, neither one touches him. When Daniel isn't watching movies with them, Oliver turns the volume so low that he and Yugo must surely hear next to nothing. The two of them huddle like mice, watching, following Daniel's movements closely from the corners of their eyes.

Yugo is getting the hang of the shopping. When he gets home from the shops or market and starts unpacking, he holds up each item tentatively, awaiting Daniel's approval. "That's fine, Yugo," Daniel says. "It's all okay." He helps pack the rest away.

They go to art exhibitions together, once to a concert. Or they go to see movies recommended by Oliver. But mostly they stay at home, behind the flat's solid nineteenth-century walls. And whenever either Oliver or Yugo goes out alone, the one left behind takes off Daniel's clothes and has sex with him.

Daniel is sitting in front of his computer. He wants to get up to turn down the thermostat—it's too hot in here—but first he needs to complete the paragraph he's writing.

Oliver approaches soundlessly from the kitchen, stands next to him. "So," he asks, "do you enjoy writing?"

At first Daniel wants to change the subject casually, but then replies all the same. "No, writing fiction is a disruptive compulsion. The last refuge of someone who cannot do anything useful." Daniel considers for a moment. "The desperate search for a gap, a chance. The taking of unquantified risks."

Oliver doesn't seem to altogether grasp Daniel's response. "But I *must* encourage you! Your story is, I think, noble! It will become a classic document! And may many more great works emerge from your pen!"

Daniel smiles mechanically at Oliver's stream of vapidities. Though perhaps no more vacuous than his own somewhat inflated reply of a moment ago. Oliver's eyes are wide; he's in the manic mood that sometimes takes hold of him while watching movies. This is the first time that Daniel has found something disturbing about his presence.

"I appreciate your optimism," Daniel says drily. "But nobility? To me it's a cold-blooded task. You forfeit a lot of your humanity in the process."

"And where does it all come from?" Oliver's eyes remain wide.

Daniel looks through the window at the buildings of the City, reflects for a moment. "Writing is in the overflow, in what follows when you think you've written yourself empty. When you've started thinking: Now I've *got* the story. When you're on the point of turning your back on the screen. *Then* it starts."

It's getting hotter and hotter in the room. Daniel feels sweat beading on his forehead. He turns to Oliver, who is frowning as if he's been subjected to the most cryptic utterance in the history of human discourse. His face is also shiny with sweat. Daniel wonders what Oliver sounds like when he's writing about cinema. When he's talking about it, his judgements are enlightening, if overexcited. Conversing with Oliver on other topics often produces an awkward caricature of a conversation.

Daniel can see that Oliver is waiting for a more palatable pronouncement. "In any case," he continues, "you may be surprised at how nonverbal the process actually is." Daniel shakes his head, as if trying to banish the subject. "Ignore what I'm saying. I'm being evasive. It's not really possible to verbalise this compulsion." He taps the computer screen. "What I do know is that sometimes an adjustment here, in the real world, can change everything *there*." He points at the screen. "I don't think the opposite is true, though."

This doesn't improve matters. Oliver is towering over him, suddenly startlingly demanding. Daniel continues helplessly. "Perhaps writing is best described as a zero-sum game. After all the effort, all the sentences, you always end up where you began. Like some empty Japanese ceremony. Meaning being as fleeting as steam."

Oliver's attention wanders. He is now focused on documents that Daniel has carelessly left lying open on the desk next to the computer. On top of the pile is a bank statement and, next to it, a printout of Daniel's latest tax return with details of his income. "Excuse the mess, Oliver." Daniel gathers the papers, puts them away in a drawer.

"Listen, I wish you the creativity of a giant! But I think you need peace," Oliver says and retreats to his and Yugo's bedroom, closing the door with a gentle click.

Daniel sits back in his chair. His concentration has been scattered beyond recall. He thinks back to two or three days before. He'd taken a shower after his and Oliver's sweat had mingled between the sheets. Yugo had gone out, mumbling some pretext or other as to where. With a towel around his waist, Daniel had come upon Oliver standing in front of his computer, scanning the text on the screen.

"I'm just looking." Oliver said. "I can't read your language." But when he walked off and Daniel closed the document, he noticed Google Translate open in the background. It was set to *Afrikaans to Serbian*. And there it was: the first page of Daniel's text, copied into the left panel.

To the right were paragraphs in Cyrillic. Heaven knows, Daniel reflected, how the American translation machine had mauled his long Afrikaans sentences. He could reverse the process, feed the gibberish back in and have it translated back to Afrikaans. Then he could have the product translated into Serbian again. And so on, to and fro. The sentences would float further and further into the unknown, the paragraphs becoming progressively more surreal. Eventually, he'd thought, he could bring into being an Afrikaans text that has next to nothing in common with his original sentences.

It is the fourth week of the Serbs' sojourn. Daniel is lying in bed with a sleeping Yugo, his body a loose heap of limbs. Daniel takes Yugo's hand, presses it to his own mouth. Yugo's fingers smell of vegetables and spices from the lunch he prepared earlier. Today they were different with each other: more intimate and trusting, more tender. Daniel doesn't want to move an inch, but he has an appointment with his friend Mirko the architect. The intercom buzzes—it's Oliver, Daniel knows. He didn't take a key. Daniel wakes Yugo gently. The Serb smiles sheepishly and stumbles half asleep to his own room to get dressed.

He meets Mirko in the café of the British Film Institute on the South Bank, tells him about the latest development with the Serbs.

His friend shakes his head. "In your flat? Just you and them? I wash my hands of it. Don't say I didn't—"

"Caution me? That's the word you keep using. A refrain. How does that help me?" Daniel says. "It's as if you know them, as if you're withholding some secret."

Mirko compresses his lips. "I have your interests at heart, believe me."

"What kind of prejudice have you got against your countrymen? Is it a class thing? Is that why you don't want to meet them?"

Mirko is still shaking his head. He pushes his wine away. "Daniel, dear Daniel. What *have* you got yourself into?"

Daniel drains his half-glass of wine in a single gulp, asks for the bill.

When Daniel gets home, the Serbs are gone. The bed in their room is neatly made. Their bags are gone, and no sign of their presence remains, no letter or note. Nothing. Or, no, there is something on the dining-room table after all. A DVD. The *Werckmeister Harmonies*, a Hungarian film about an isolated village that is visited by a circus exhibiting a dead whale.

The Serbs have left no new contact details. The numbers saved in Daniel's phone are linked to temporary British SIM cards. He tries Oliver's number straight away. It no longer functions. He has only an email address for Yugo, and the morning after their departure he writes to him: *Don't you say goodbye?* It bounces back.

The next month Daniel spends largely in front of his computer screen—the cursor constantly blinking in the same place mocks him, his hands are paralysed. Suddenly it is spring, he realises one morning; blossoms have appeared overnight. He opens a window, inhales the city's scents.

On a whim, he picks up his phone, scrolls down to his father's number. The last call (made, not received, like all the calls in the log) was almost a year ago, he notices. He imagines the old man in his enormous suburban house in Cape Town, alone amid Daniel's dead mother's art collection. Cape Town's autumn breezes would be moving across the vast and silent lawn, making the water in the pool, which no-one has entered for a quarter-century, shiver. He scrolls down further, to his sister's number. She lives an hour away from his father, in the gentle hills of the winelands. She's harder to picture. Dressed in linen, Daniel imagines, make-up matched to the season's colours. In the cool leather seat of a car, or having breakfast among vineyards. He doesn't call anyone, puts the phone in his pocket.

He leaves the flat, goes to see a new exhibition at the Tate Modern. French pop art from the sixties and seventies. It's feeble—the one genre in which the Americans surpass the continental artists. At Borough Market he buys ingredients for a solo meal, tries preparing one of Yugo's recipes from memory. Then one day he goes to the nearest Sainsbury's and buys the kind of stuff that Yugo would have bought—processed meat and sausages, sliced sweetmilk cheese, cans of sliced peaches in syrup probably sweet enough to scald your throat. Daniel unpacks it all in rows on his dining-room table. He eats none of it, dumps it in the bin.

* * *

Daniel receives an email from Oliver. He shakes his head at the address: *wildserbiandog@gmail.com*. And at the contents. It's as if Oliver has made an effort to write in a manner he imagines is expected of him. The presumed conventions, however, are obscure to Daniel. The tone—and the odd English—remind Daniel of the shysters who send out missives to tens of thousands of people in a scam to cheat one or two idiots. But Oliver does not ask for money, and promises nothing.

Greetings, true Friend! he opens. Daniel scan-reads. Further along, the Serb writes: *So this is my Invitation to you, my generous Friend. Let us have a Reunion! And we choose*

Germany!! There is not a word in the letter about their stay with him in London or their abrupt departure.

In florid style and illogical capitalising, Oliver sets out his plan for the three of them to travel to a relatively unvisited part of Southern Germany. It's reminiscent of the promotional material of an inept travel agent. *The views are Enchanting!! The rushing rivers even refreshing for Summer swims!* Oliver has already fixed the dates. He and Yugo have booked a bus from Belgrade, and he suggests a specific flight for Daniel. From Gatwick, touching down in one of those airports in the middle of nowhere, served exclusively by budget airlines. And they've booked rooms in a youth hostel. *Until we meet again, Friend!*

Daniel ponders for a while, then books an airline ticket. The weekend selected by the Serbs is the cheapest one all summer. *You will see,* Oliver writes. *I have planned it all Professionally!* Daniel does not reply. Not yet. He'll decide later whether to actually use the ticket.

They meet in the street in front of the hostel. Oliver and Yugo are sitting on a bench next to the entrance, evidently waiting for him. Daniel has never let them know that he was coming, imagining what a big surprise it would be if he simply turned up.

"Have you rented a car?" is Oliver's first surly question. Before saying hello. He seems, to Daniel's bafflement, not at all surprised by his arrival. Yugo gives Daniel a hug and a resounding kiss and then Oliver remembers to do the same. Their physical engagement with Daniel in each other's presence takes him unawares. "Wait, I forget, we have to show you your room." Oliver takes Daniel's case, drags him inside by the arm.

As they walk past the reception desk, an acned young

German greets them. "Oh yes," Oliver says to Daniel, "you must still pay." For all three of them, it would seem. The other two have been allowed to check in on the promise that Daniel would come to settle the bill.

"The car?" Oliver demands curtly once Daniel has paid. Daniel tries in vain to reconcile this new tone with that of Oliver's email.

"I took a taxi here, but we could rent a car if necessary..."

"It's necessary!" Oliver says, smiling. "We're going to be walking *and* driving, you'll see."

The village is on a tear-shaped river island. There are only a few other tourists in the hostel, and apparently few other travellers elsewhere in the village. The hostel faces an uninspiring little park jutting out at an acute angle into the river— the sharp point of the tear. They walk through the village, looking for an eatery. Oliver and Yugo select one that serves heavy Southern German dishes. Halfway through the meal, Daniel lowers his soup spoon—still holding a dumpling—to gaze in amazement at the other two eating like wolves. They order more, devour platefuls. It's as if they're feeding for the first time in weeks. Their faces, Daniel realises, are leaner than before. For a moment he feels something like fatherly concern for them. Yugo looks up with a spot of gravy on his chin, grins boyishly.

When Daniel wakes up the next morning and knocks sleepily at the Serbs' bedroom door, there is no answer. He opens the door; it's not locked. Their backpacks are arranged neatly by the window, in the sunlight, but the Serbs are gone. Daniel goes to have breakfast, then sits down outside the hostel, looking out over the little park. *Das Dorf der drei Flüsse*, he reads in a brochure he took from the hostel's reception desk. The village of three rivers. You can tell from the clothing of the people in the photos that they were taken in the seventies. He gets up and walks through the park to the point of the island, like the prow of a ship. From both sides, smaller rivers debouch into the larger.

Daniel turns when he hears his name. Oliver and Yugo are waving furiously from the hostel entrance. "We've found a tent!" Oliver shouts.

Daniel walks back to them. "A tent? I didn't know we were looking for one."

"For our hiking trip, of course!"

They lead Daniel to a shop selling camping equipment, where a special three-person tent, apparently designed for polar conditions, is available. They place it on the counter, together with a small gas stove and other basic camping gear. Daniel pays.

"Definitely one for the serious camper," the shop assistant says as he hands over the tent.

"We are serious," Yugo confirms immediately. In London he seldom said anything, but here on the continent he has evidently found his voice.

"Now we won't care if the world ends," says Oliver as they leave. "Now we are prepared for anything."

"Avalanches and mudslides," Yugo says.

"Monsoons and rock falls," Oliver says.

"It's summer," Daniel says. "Snow is unlikely. And we're not in the Alps or Andes or Amazon. I think we should be safe."

"Safe," says Yugo, flashing his ironic glance in Oliver's direction.

"Safe," Oliver echoes and laughs, displaying his golden teeth. They exchange a few words in Serbian.

They plan on spending three nights at the campsite. Staying in the most expensive hotel in town would probably have been cheaper than buying such a sophisticated tent, Daniel thinks. They're travelling in a car he rented in the village early that morning. They struggle to find the campsite. The car's navigation system orders them in peremptory German to turn off onto a dirt road straggling up a hill. The road leads to a dusty parking area next to a precipice. From here there's a fine view over the village with its confluence of three rivers. The navigation system does not acknowledge the rock face falling away before the front wheels. A female voice orders them in curt German to carry on driving, as if they could seamlessly continue along the roads far beneath them.

They ignore the instruction, turn round, drive back. The voice insists repeatedly that they should make a U-turn as soon as possible and launch themselves off the cliff. "Murderous, isn't she, this Fräulein in the machine?" Daniel says, laughing. The two gaze at him as if he's said something insulting.

At last, with the aid of Google Maps on Daniel's phone, they find the campsite. It is clearly not a popular spot. There's only a single other tent, in the far corner of the site.

They were supposed to start walking today, but all the driving around has been time-consuming; it's early afternoon already. They'd also stopped to buy liquor on the way. A plethora of cheap beer. Oliver had placed it on the counter, waiting for Daniel to pay.

Now they sit down around a non-existent campfire. Each opens a cold can and starts drinking. Oliver arranges the unopened cans of beer in a pyramid.

Daniel declines a second beer. "Are you sure?" Oliver says. "We've just started!" The two Serbs laugh in sync, open more cans. The two lie with their backs against their backpacks, arses in the dust, drinking. They're speaking Serbian now. Daniel opens a bottle of water. The Serbs look at the bottle, then at each other, erupting in laughter.

"What's so funny?"

They shake their heads, full of stifled laughter. "You Brits!" Oliver says.

"You'll recall, I'm actually not a Brit."

"You're our friend, Daniel, you're our friend. That's what counts. Whether you come from here or there. England or Africa, Budapest or Vladivostok. You're still our guy." They laugh again. Yugo rolls over, his head resting on Oliver's chest, spilling beer on himself. They open more beers. They keep offering Daniel cans from the pyramid, growing more insistent the more inebriated they become. He just shakes his head.

With the beer they also bought a lot of tinned food. Daniel wanted to suggest some other items, but eventually just shrugged, let them be. After a couple of hours of drinking, Daniel offers to prepare food. By now he's lost count of the beers the two Serbs have guzzled—the pinnacle of the beer pyramid has been imbibed; the base is also starting to erode. But Yugo insists on preparing the meal himself. He struggles for a while to light the gas stove. Then he upends cans of food—incompatible ingredients—into a saucepan on the stove and starts mixing them. He spills baked beans onto the flame, producing a strong smell of scorching. He pours some beer into the mix, then takes a sip from the can and spits an arc of the liquid straight into the saucepan. Oliver laughs. Yugo sits down hard on the ground, smiles broadly at Daniel, shaking his head.

"You're a funny one, Daniel," Yugo says. "With all your manners. All your privileges." Yugo tenses his face, rolls back his eyes, stiffens his upper lip. An imitation, apparently, of Daniel's imputed affectation. "Makes you wonder." What it makes one wonder is not clear to Daniel, but he doesn't ask.

Yugo takes the saucepan off the stove before it's steaming properly and ladles spoonfuls of the concoction into three mugs. Daniel has to grab his arm when he almost stumbles into the flame of the stove.

The food is lukewarm. The two Serbs carry on drinking as they eat. Then they stagger to the tent, lie down. Oliver summons Daniel from inside. For a while he remains sitting outside, indecisive. The voice comes again, lazy but imperious. Daniel gets up and crawls into the tent, zips up the flap. It's late afternoon. The heat of the day has accumulated in the tent; it's stifling. Alcohol fumes hang heavily under the canvas. For the first time the two of them undress Daniel together, one on either side of him. They kiss him sloppily, their bodies clumsy and pressing. Their onslaughts are rougher than in the past. Daniel smells the beer and butane gas on their skins, the sweat in armpits. When Oliver's body, after a short while, shudders with joy or fury, he says something in English that Daniel can't immediately grasp. After Yugo has also ejaculated, the Serbs fall asleep without ceremony. Daniel also drops off, despite their snoring and the fumes.

Daniel wakes up with something damp and warm beneath him. Oliver is lying against his back, his arm flung heavily over Daniel. Yugo's buttocks are against Daniel's stomach. Daniel disentangles himself with difficulty. There is a large wet patch on the red sleeping bag. Oliver has urinated in his sleep.

"Shit!" Daniel exclaims loudly. The other two don't stir in their stupor. Wrapping a towel around his waist, Daniel walks to the shower block in the early dusk. Somebody's shaving at one of the basins, in fierce electric light. A wiry young man wearing only football shorts. While Daniel is showering in the open shower area, he inspects the tattoo on the young man's back. He recognises the emblem on his flanks, a two-headed eagle, as an element of the Serbian flag. How can there be another Serb here? And the only other camper, too. Could this be a popular destination for tourists from Belgrade? The man takes no notice of Daniel, just carries on shaving till his fingertips glide smoothly over his cheeks. Then he turns round. While now gazing unabashedly at Daniel, he lowers his Adidas shorts. He leaves them right there on the floor, his gaze still on Daniel, the penis smooth and swarthy and uncut. Daniel shuts down his own shower, goes to dry himself next to the crumpled shorts. The Serb turns on his shower. Daniel fixes his gaze on the coal-black pubic hair and suddenly realises what it was that Oliver had shouted earlier when ropes of semen whipped from his groin. "Everybody gets broken!" Something like that. And moments later, muttering in his convulsions: "Sooner or later."

When Daniel returns, both Serbs have woken up. They're surly and befuddled with beer and sleep. Together they eat the half-congealed leftovers and go to bed early. All three in a row, as before, the damp bedding now removed. As they press up against him from both sides, still not quite sober, Daniel can feel how bony they've become. Each is still as tall as before, almost a head taller than he, but they're considerably thinner now. The soups and dumplings and wodges of pork of the last few days in the Dorf der drei Flüsse have not yet managed to put flesh on their bones.

Heat builds up during the night. Breath from three mouths condenses against the canvas, drips on Daniel's repose.

The two wake up with bloodshot eyes. They don't seem particularly keen on hiking. Daniel packs a rucksack nevertheless, and after a greasy breakfast from tins, they depart.

The Serbs are sullen, drink a lot of water, stop every twenty minutes to urinate. The route is not spectacular, but pleasant. They're surprised when they end up at the same observation point where they stopped the car the previous day. From here you can see the whole village—the tear-shaped island, the roofs of the houses, the youth hostel, the drab little park. The three rivers flowing together in a white turbulence.

They walk back. Around noon, the sun scorching their sweaty shoulders, all three of them shirtless, Oliver suddenly comes to a halt. Daniel almost crashes into him from behind. Oliver's breathing accelerates. He leaves the path, stumbles a few steps, bends over in the grass. Yugo, who's some distance ahead, trots back and puts his arm around Oliver's hunched shoulders. Oliver's body convulses, as if he's going to vomit. Nothing happens.

"Are you okay?" Daniel asks uncertainly from a distance.

Oliver slowly straightens and turns around. A long string of saliva is dangling from his lip, glinting in the sun. Pale and silent, he observes Daniel.

The two Serbs walk ahead. Neither of them looks back, neither says another word.

When they return, the other camper has left; their hired car is the only one left in the camping ground. Getting closer, they see that their own three-person tent is also gone.

Oliver stops in his tracks. "Fucking Serb!" he shouts. "I knew we couldn't trust him!"

It's not only the tent that's been stolen. They do a quick inventory, trying to establish what's missing. The valuable items—phones and wallets—they had with them. Daniel's computer was locked in the car. But the gas stove and their food are gone. So are the sleeping bags and their best clothes.

"He'll probably sell the stuff for fuck-all to some pawn

shop in Belgrade!" Oliver lowers his voice menacingly: "If he was still here we'd burn down his tent. With him inside."

"Or," says Yugo, "drown him in his own piss." Daniel turns to him. He wonders if he's been misreading Yugo's amiable grin all along. Furious saliva has gathered in the corners of the Serb's mouth.

They drive back to the village, to the youth hostel. After only one night in the hills. How, Daniel wonders as he drives, did Oliver know the other camper was a Serb? It's conceivable, he supposes, that he also saw the back tattoo.

Oliver's mood has darkened since the theft. Over supper in the village of three rivers he suggests that they cut short their time in Germany and take a bus back to Belgrade—and that Daniel come along for a visit.

"We'll show you our life."

"I have to get back to London. There are things I have to do, deadlines looming. I doubt my return flight is refundable. And at some stage I also have to visit South Africa, for a change. I haven't seen my family in—"

"You're rich, aren't you." Oliver's voice is cutting. "You can easily book a new flight from Belgrade."

"I wouldn't exactly call myself rich," Daniel says emphatically. "I could, I suppose, book another flight—"

"There you are, then it's all agreed!" Yugo says, once again his imperturbably good-natured self.

The overnight bus departs from a terminal in Nuremberg. In the late afternoon they return the car in the village and take a taxi to the terminal. The bus ride takes almost twelve hours. There was a daytime bus, but Oliver booked this one because it was cheaper. They travel in darkness through Austria, Slovenia, and Bosnia and Herzegovina. Daniel sees hardly anything of the landscapes, only the brightly lit shops of the service stations where they stop a few times. None of them sleep. At last the bus enters the Serbian dawn.

From the Belgrade bus terminal they take a taxi to the outskirts. Daniel pays. The concrete building in which Oliver and Yugo live is one of three parallel blocks. Grey and dreary—housing from the communist era that isn't monumental enough to attain ironic value.

The two Serbs let Daniel lead the way into the flat. The interior is from the seventies, perhaps early eighties. Patterned wallpaper, a brown carpet, decorative beams under the ceiling. In the corner of the living room is an old-fashioned woodburning stove with glazed tiles. It's out of keeping with the modern building and takes up a good quarter of the room.

The Serbs put down their backpacks. Oliver spreads his arms wide, one hand nearly grazing Daniel's cheek. "Our home," he says, "is your home. Please indulge fully in our hospitality. Eat what you like, friend, and come and go as you please." Oliver's voice is weary. He doesn't sound convinced by his own generosity.

There's only one bedroom. Daniel is assigned the sofa in the cramped living room. They all take a nap, catching up a few hours of the night's lost sleep. When they wake in the late afternoon, they eat the sandwiches they bought on the bus trip. They watch television until dark, until they grow sleepy again and start preparing for bed.

Daniel has to pass through the bedroom to get to the bathroom. The Serbs are brushing their teeth. Daniel waits behind them, then brushes his own teeth over the foamy saliva in the basin, streaked pink with traces of gum blood.

When Daniel emerges from the bathroom, they're in bed already, sitting upright next to each other, legs outstretched, watching him. He expects them to invite him, that they'll make space between them. They don't budge. Daniel lingers, goes up to the foot of the bed. Lightly, he touches Yugo's sock. Yugo withdraws his toes.

"Do you need another blanket, perhaps?" Oliver asks.

"Do you want to make yourself some herbal tea before you go to bed?" Yugo enquires.

Inside the flat it's as hot as it was outside earlier, too oppressive for even the thin sheet that Oliver gave Daniel. And Daniel isn't thirsty. "No," he says, "I'm okay." He yawns exaggeratedly. "Good night," he says, open-mouthed. He leaves, pulling the door shut.

The sofa sags under his hip when he lies down, and the armrest butts against his head. Now and again a man shouts in the street, or elsewhere in the building. A car's tyres skid over tar in the distance. Daniel fancies that the attention of the occupants of all the flats has imperceptibly shifted to him, lying here. He pulls the sheet over his head, yanks it off again when it gets too hot. It takes him a long time to fall asleep.

Daniel wakes up early. The Serbs haven't stirred. He goes out, walks a few blocks, to a street where he noticed a row of shops on arrival yesterday. Teenage boys with shaved skulls and football shirts are lounging on the pavement, leaning against a wall. They blow smoke at him languidly as he walks past. One spits on the ground. Daniel buys eggs and bread in a small convenience store.

Back at the flat, there's still no sign of life from the bedroom. He prepares breakfast—French toast. He's forgotten to buy syrup, but finds a bottle in a kitchen cupboard, encrusted around the cap. He manages, with an effort, to open it, sniffs it. Maple syrup, though artificially flavoured. He drizzles it on the egg-soaked bread. He makes herbal tea, arranges everything neatly on a tray. Resting the tray on one raised knee, he knocks on the bedroom door. No reaction. Daniel enters. Both men are sitting upright in their bed in the semi-darkness, just as he left them the night before. As if silently awaiting him. They look as if they've been awake for a long time. Or haven't slept at all. Daniel puts down the tray.

The Serbs look at the tray, then at each other. "That's not what we usually have for breakfast," Oliver says and shakes his head.

"Good morning," Daniel says. He can't make out whether they're implying it's a wrong choice or a pleasant surprise. They don't seem particularly hungry or interested in the food.

With something of his usual mischievous tone, Yugo says: "Morning. That's a breakfast for a giant!"

"With giant flavour, I'm sure." Oliver looks down while he's speaking. He sounds subdued. Daniel goes to open the curtains.

"No," Oliver says. He raises a hand to screen the light from his eyes. "No! Too much sun. Keep it closed." It's dull and overcast outside, but Daniel closes the curtains again.

There isn't a second tray. Daniel brings his own plate, sits on the edge of the bed and starts eating. The Serbs pick at their food without enthusiasm.

They eat in silence for a while. Then Daniel looks up. "I've been wanting to ask you since Germany: Why did you leave my place in London so suddenly?"

Oliver prods at the bread with his fork. "An emergency. There was no other way."

Daniel waits, but there's no follow-up. "Nothing I did, I hope . . . ?"

"No," Oliver says again, shaking his head decisively. "You were a true friend and host. Just an emergency."

Then Daniel notices Yugo's nails. They're painted black.

Daniel is sure they weren't like that yesterday on the bus. And they were definitely not black in Germany.

Daniel points at the nails with his fork. "I see you're a gay Serbian goth now," he says teasingly. Yugo and Oliver look at each other, frowning, then redirect their gaze slowly at Daniel. They are not amused. Daniel feels his own smile fade.

Oliver takes Yugo's hand, examines the nails as if seeing the polish for the first time. He lifts the hand, kisses it, presses it to his breast. "He is not a goth," Oliver says. "Has never been." He sounds insulted, hurt.

Daniel lifts an apologetic hand. "Sorry, just joking. I didn't mean anything by it."

Something, Daniel thinks, is out of kilter. The air in here is starved of oxygen. And it's as if all three of them are saying their sentences backwards.

Daniel imagines that the two will take him on a tour of the city after breakfast, that they'll do the tourist rounds together. He waits patiently, while the Serbs shower and dress at a leisurely pace, for them to reveal the day's activities.

He is mistaken. They remain idling, don't seem to have planned any excursion. At length he says to Yugo: "Don't you want to show me round the neighbourhood?" He hopes this will prompt Yugo to offer to show him the city. Yugo just nods.

Oliver shakes his head when Daniel invites him along: "No time, dishes to wash." His eyes remain cast down and his voice sounds more and more strained.

Daniel and Yugo walk to the street where Daniel bought food earlier, and do a few turns around the neighbourhood. The only sights are more blocks of flats like the one they're staying in. There are some shops advertising lottery tickets, a few cars with squealing tyres, youths in tracksuit pants and baseball caps kicking soccer balls in the streets. Daniel glances back at one young man who fists the palm of his hand as he walks. He could swear it's the guy with the Serbian flag on his back, the one who stole their things in Germany. He meets Daniel's gaze, grinning, shoulder muscles tensed against his T-shirt.

"Do you know him?" Daniel asks Yugo. He imagines he saw the two exchange almost imperceptible nods.

"Everybody knows everybody here!"

As they turn a corner, a soccer ball hits Daniel full on the temple. He staggers back, but stays on his feet. Blood surges in his head. A smooth-skinned sixteen or seventeen-year-old boy comes trotting up. He raises a hand, shouts something apologetically. Yugo picks up the ball, stands waiting for the boy to reach him. Then he lifts his hand and gives the young man a slap on the head that makes his teeth rattle. Daniel gasps, his mouth dropping open. He looks from the boy to Yugo. When the boy regains his balance, there are tears in his eyes. In a voice Daniel's never heard before, Yugo berates him in Serbian. Then Yugo walks on, Daniel following at his heels.

"He needed that," Yugo says. "Needs to be educated." He smiles, his normal voice now restored. "We're all like parents here. The whole village." What village the Serb is referring to remains obscure to Daniel. And does *anybody* practise parenting here? Daniel says nothing, just replays the moment of violence again and again in his head. He looks at Yugo, or whoever is really walking next to him—Yugo, whom he thought he knew.

They go straight home after the slap. Oliver is sitting in front of the television. He's bundled Daniel's pillow and sheet to one side on the sofa.

"How was it?" Oliver asks, his eyes still on the TV.

"A pleasant neighbourhood," Daniel comments feebly.

The Serbs both shake their heads. Yugo says something in Serbian. "Yes," says Oliver in English, apparently in reply. "Exactly."

"What is he saying?" Daniel wants to know.

"He says the place isn't pleasant, it's a shithole," says Oliver. "If you want a direct translation: 'The place where the wolves mate.' That's what it is. This city, this street. This flat. This sofa we're sitting on."

"But it's your place. It's where you live."

"No," Yugo says, his mouth tight. "It's got nothing to do with us." There's a new vehemence in the way he shakes his head.

Yugo sits down next to Oliver on the sofa. Daniel takes the floor. Oliver flips through the channels, lands on an American documentary. It's about a couple who kept their thirteen children shackled in the basement of their home for two decades. The children were treated like dogs, kept in filthy conditions, undernourished. They were eventually discovered and rescued. A doctor explains that some of the children were so underdeveloped that they looked a decade younger than their true age.

Oliver sits transfixed. The kind of manic commentary that he sometimes delivered when watching films in London is absent.

Daniel looks at the shelf of DVDs next to the sofa. He went through them the night before: an impressive collection of mainly Central and Eastern European films, as well as some Russian. He'd rather watch one of those.

Oliver's now watching some kind of Eastern European singing contest. The living-room curtains are almost completely closed, the blue light of the television illuminating the Serbs' faces. Oliver looks serious, his skin stretched tight across his skull.

Daniel is impossibly tired. He takes his bedding from the sofa, spreads it on the carpet under the window and lies down. The last thing he sees on the screen, before dropping off, is a corpulent teenage Hungarian boy in a white leather jacket singing a Whitney Houston number. Oliver's gaze does not stray for one second from the screen.

Daniel wakes up with Yugo shaking him by the shoulder. It's early evening, almost dusk. Oliver's still in the same spot, his eyes glued to the television. He's watching a programme about the worst storms in American history. Scene after scene of cars careening on frozen freeways.

Yugo places a plate in front of Daniel: a sandwich and an apple. He's ravenous and devours the sandwich in half a minute, then the apple. He wipes juice from his chin, still hungry. Oliver and Yugo eat something else, a kind of stew. Nobody says anything. On the television a truck jack-knifes across four lanes. Three cars collide.

Oliver, evidently bored, surfs the channels, touching down on a nature programme. After all the trash TV, this grabs Daniel's attention. Along with Oliver, he sits riveted. A donkey and two wolves come across each other in the wild. The wolves have never seen a donkey and vice versa. The donkey pricks up his ears; he starts to flee. The silver-toothed wolves follow him. But then the donkey slows down, stops. The wolves stop in turn, suddenly full of doubt. The donkey starts walking purposefully towards the wolves. The wolves retreat, in case the donkey's teeth are more formidable than their own. The donkey speeds up, starts chasing the wolves. The wolves are now running at full speed, for dear life.

After supper the Serbs go to their room. As Daniel drifts off, he wonders why he's here, somewhere on the outskirts of Belgrade, in the company of these two increasingly morose and remote men. Here in the half-light of the television, in the exhausted mustiness of concrete. What is he to make of the days in this place, so alien and monotonous, the purposelessness of everything? How has he ended up here, and what on god's earth is keeping him here?

Unexpectedly, he feels a yearning for Cape Town. For South Africa. The country that has always felt like a strange wind on his skin. And that harbours a father whose presence penetrates to even the oddest corners of the world. He is here now, the old man. He has arrived: seeping from the concrete like an odour from a rigid corpse.

Daniel is woken up by the sounds of Yugo preparing breakfast—French toast. Daniel gets up from the sofa, rubs his eyes. "I thought you didn't eat French toast."

Yugo doesn't look up from the pan. "It's for you."

Daniel points at a box of cereal on the table. Multicoloured sugared hoops. Children's food. "Is *that* what you're going to eat?"

Yugo shakes his head. "Today we're eating nothing." He touches his belly. "Our stomachs are not feeling well. By the way, don't open the door for anybody when you're on your own here. And keep the curtains closed."

Daniel fails to see how he might ever be on his own. Apart from Yugo's little outing with him, the Serbs have not ventured out once. Daniel looks at the curtains, then down at his laptop on the floor. Since leaving England he hasn't touched it, not written a word. It lies in wait like a trap on the feculent carpet.

The intercom sounds; without asking who it is, Yugo presses the button to unlock the street door. A short while later there's a knock at the front door. Oliver emerges from the bedroom. His hair is mussed, his eyes red.

"We thought we'd introduce you," he says, sleep-befuddled,

as he opens the door. He points at the woman standing there. "My mother!" he says, as if announcing a royal entrance.

Daniel is still in the boxer shorts he slept in, has just thrown on a T-shirt. "An unexpected pleasure to meet you." He shakes her hand.

She doesn't speak a word of English, it turns out. Daniel recalls, back in London, Oliver talking about his mother as a free spirit. Inconceivable that the woman before him once was a proponent of free love, of festivals in the forests, of moonlit revels. She looks like a frumpish Serbian matriarch, albeit dressed like a teenager.

They sit in silence at the table. Daniel eats his French toast; the other three drink herbal tea. Oliver nudges Daniel with his elbow, winks. "What do you think of my mother? A real hippie, eh?"

Daniel nods, frowning. He looks at the woman next to him, at her sun-ravaged skin and wine-red hair, at her white lycra slacks and the silver sandals she's discarded at the front door. "A real hippie, yes, Oliver." Smiling, the woman lights a cigarette.

Daniel wonders whether the two Serbs, these men whom he cannot let go, have fathers. Neither of them has ever mentioned one.

Oliver's mother leaves in the late morning. At Daniel's request, Yugo supplies him with a map of Belgrade's city centre. Yugo doesn't offer to accompany him, but points out a few landmarks and attractions, explains the transport system. He gives Daniel a key so he can come and go as he pleases.

Outside, Daniel walks past the stop where buses leave for the city centre. He wanders aimlessly, feeling the eyes of young men on him. If he didn't know better, he would take their gazes for desire. He googles "gay Belgrade" on his phone. The city has queer bars and a gay nightclub or two. It can surely not be as homophobic as Oliver and Yugo described it.

Is he imagining things, wandering the streets, or have the adolescent boys all come to a standstill? They regard him in silence, biceps tensed, skins fuming with adrenaline. It's as if they know who he is, and that he doesn't belong here. When he walks past one group, they all take a step or two towards him. Daniel's heart starts thumping. He keeps his gaze down, but from the corner of his eye he sees that the leader of the pack is the one who looks like the guy who robbed them. Time to get back to the flat.

In his haste he takes a wrong turn, has to turn back. The streets are filling up with gangs of youths, as if he attracts them like a magnet. All eyes are on him, or that's how it feels. He picks up his pace, starts jogging. When he reaches the flat and turns the key in the front door, his hands are trembling.

Silence reigns. Daniel knocks at the bedroom door, pushes it ajar. The curtains are drawn. The two Serbs are lying in the dimness. They're not feeling well, says Yugo—stomach cramps. They don't ask him why he's returned so soon.

"Can I go and buy you something? Medicine?"

Yugo seems to nod.

"Do you want to give me a list? I don't know brand names."

Yugo sighs, reaches for a sheet of paper, writes down a few items in the semi-darkness.

Daniel takes a deep breath before stepping out into the street. He fixes his eyes on the pavement, ignoring the bands of young men. He walks to the street with the shops, finds a pharmacy. The pharmacist asks questions in Serbian about his list. Daniel lifts his shoulders. The pharmacist loses patience, pushes a few bottles into his hands. Only two of them correspond to the names on the list. Anti-nausea medication, as far as Daniel can ascertain from Google, and rehydration solution.

Opening the flat door, Daniel hears somebody vomiting in the bathroom. The bedroom door is ajar; he pushes it open. Oliver is lying on the bed, watching Yugo, who's crouched by the toilet.

"Everything okay?"

"What does it look like?" Oliver demands. "We're as sick as fucking dogs. And it's from that food you gave us!"

Daniel is taken aback. "The French toast? From yesterday morning? I'm sorry if that's so, Oliver, but I doubt it. I ate it myself and I'm fine. Also, it's probably too long ago. In the meantime you've eaten all sorts of other—"

"It's from your food. That toast you fed us." There is naked malice in his voice. Daniel is speechless.

The two Serbs take turns to vomit violently. Sounds and smells emanate from the bedroom. Oliver refuses to have any windows open, shouts at Daniel angrily when he tries to slide open the living-room window surreptitiously. It becomes unendurable. Daniel goes out again, braving the stares on the street. There are now fewer teenagers moving about. He buys white bread, a packet of powdered soup. Perhaps Oliver and Yugo will eat something later on.

Back in the flat things have calmed down; there is silence in the bedroom. Daniel prepares toast and soup, opens the bedroom door a crack and slides it in. The other two are asleep, he imagines. Daniel lies down too, drops off.

Daniel wakes to Oliver calling from the bedroom. He takes up position outside their door, knocks hesitantly. "Come in!" they say in unison.

"You've saved our lives, Daniel," says Oliver. He looks

haggard, though less disgruntled than in the previous few days. They're sitting up, eating the toast.

Daniel shrugs. "I didn't do much."

Oliver asks Daniel to open the curtains. He does so, letting in the light.

"Listen, we must ask you something," Yugo says. "Come, sit down here." He pats the bed with his palm. Daniel sits down gingerly. "Something we've been wanting to know for a long time." He looks round the room. "This flat." He waits for a moment. "We're going to lose it."

"Except," says Oliver, "if you help us. Except if you buy it for us."

Daniel is caught unawares. Once again speechless.

"I can see you think it's expensive," says Oliver. He looks down, shakes his head; his voice accelerates. "It's not expensive. Not at all. It costs not even forty thousand pounds."

They've stopped eating. They're watching him. It occurs to Daniel that perhaps somehow they made themselves ill, that it was all a device to break down his defences, to soften him up.

Daniel takes a deep breath, looks down at the bedding. "I think . . . you're under a misapprehension . . . I'm afraid you have the wrong idea about my financial means."

"Please, Daniel," Yugo says. He looks pale, lying there in the light. "We know you can."

"I can't, Yugo." Daniel looks at him. "I can help you with a thousand pounds or so. But I have my own obligations. I definitely don't have that kind of money. There is no way I can buy you a home. I'm sorry if you were under a different impression."

Daniel gets to his feet. Without looking back at them, he walks out into the living room. He switches on the television, gazes at it unseeingly for a while. He has to get out. He can't stay here for a moment longer, in this space smelling of vomit. He switches off the TV, peers into the bedroom. The two are sitting bolt upright in bed like wax dolls. "I'm going to see the sights," he says, trying to sound cheerful. "Tourist stuff." Yugo hardly looks up, lifts a hand in half-hearted greeting.

In the bus, on his way to the city centre, Daniel feels, for the first time in a long while, that he's breathing clean air. Light streams in through the window. He tilts his head back as if the sun has never shone on his cheeks before. In the city centre he wanders about aimlessly, has a coffee, looks at a few buildings. He checks Google again, tracks down one of the gay bars, has a beer there. The windows are painted black, like in 1980s London. It's dim inside.

How did he end up in the lives of these two people? Did he have a say in it? Has it been in any way a matter of will?

It's late afternoon when he gets off the bus. The teenagers are out on the streets. Are there no *girls* in this neighbourhood? Is it the showing off that scares them off—the recklessness on bicycles and skateboards, the back-to-front baseball caps, the glistening sweat? You might think that this was a colony exclusively for fit teenage boys, that nobody else is permitted to live here. A place where younger boys are raised and initiated by the older ones, and where you're quietly smothered in your bed on the morning of your twentieth birthday.

Crouching on the pavement in front of him is a boy who looks younger, or at any rate leaner, than the rest. He's the only one who isn't part of a group. He is bent over, examining something. Daniel slows his pace as he walks past. In the boy's hand is a tiny bird. Daniel can't be sure, but he thinks it's the boy that Yugo slapped so hard. After another few paces Daniel suddenly feels weak, drained. He stops, half closing his eyes. All that remains of this afternoon are a few light grey streaks on the horizon, like a minimalist painting. Apart from that, only the bodies speeding past on bicycles or skateboards in the turbid light, and, behind him, two warm boyish palms and a naked fledgling cheeping as if it's being murdered.

He walks on, slowing down as he approaches the building. His feet drag up the stairs. He listens with his ear to the door of the flat. Silence. He turns the key in the lock, opens the door. The living-room curtains are open for the first time. The room has an unearthly smell. On the floor is a toppled dining-room chair. And there, against the bright light, Oliver and Yugo are hanging. Round the neck of each is a belt (Daniel recognises both as his), tied to a ceiling beam. Their heads loll forward, the crowns touching. Oliver's arm is resting loosely on Yugo's shoulder: They must have embraced each other as one of them kicked over the chair.

* * *

Daniel feels as if he is only now coming back to himself, sitting in this old Eastern Block police station, facing a shaven-headed detective who swivels his chair and narrows his eyes in a manifest effort to intimidate him. Daniel thinks back to every decision, every action that took him from London to Germany, to a campsite hidden in the hills, and then to the here and now in Belgrade. Did a kind of trance take possession of him, a swoon transport him away? His brain is now emerging from the fog, into a clearer space.

The police detective across the desk questions Daniel about all these things. These are questions that can't lead anywhere, or at least can illuminate nothing for a detective: how and where he met Oliver and Yugo, when he came to

Serbia, what he came here to do. What the nature of the relationships was—Oliver and Yugo's, and Daniel's with them. Daniel's British passport lies in the centre of the wide desk. Now and again the policeman rests a heavy hand on it. The performance is transparent, modelled on a hard-baked interrogator in an American crime thriller. Diagonally behind Daniel stands a woman who interprets laboriously. Daniel projects a sardonic smile across the desk, answers only the odd question and then in very few words. Asked what he's been doing in Belgrade over the last few days, he replies: "Waiting. Seeing what would happen."

"Are you aware," the policeman continues, his eyes like gimlets, "that the two deceased were in serious financial straits?" The policeman leans forward, the better to serve up the main drama. "And did you know that the deceased have been sought for quite some time for using counterfeit cheques? And that also in England there are fraud charges pending against them?" Settling his elbows on the table, he waits a moment. "And perhaps you were part of the whole outfit. A member of their ring. Are you, Mr. Daniel, the British link in the chain?"

Daniel laughs, shaking his head. "What? People still use *cheques* here?" He adds: "Daniel is my first name*,* incidentally, not my surname." He is not anxious. He doesn't have to say much. He knows he's not in trouble, especially not as a British citizen. This policeman's game is almost played out, and then he, Mr. Daniel, will calmly board a flight to London.

His reflections do cast a backward beam, though. What fantasies of risk-taking had he cherished? What malign plot had he expected from the Serbs? That they were planning to get him drunk on cheap beer there in the German campsite, and then murder him gruesomely? That the other Serbian camper, the one with the impossibly black pubic hair, was their accomplice, and that it would be his task to carve Daniel up? That they'd hide the body parts somewhere in those peaceful hills, in plastic bags twisted closed with wire? That Oliver and Yugo would have emptied his bank accounts long before the police could connect his teeth with his dental records? But that their young fellow camper, after meeting Daniel's gaze in the shower, couldn't follow through—that he played a trick on Oliver and Yugo, chose to steal what he could and cleared out?

Previously, in London, Daniel had harboured dark suspicions, spawned by the kind of prejudices that your average Brit might harbour, such as the possibility that the couple were war criminals. But mainly he'd thought—hoped—that they would bring some colour into his days and shock his fiction into a new direction. That ultimately he'd be able to move them around like pawns. Or possessions.

The policeman picks up the red passport, flips through it. "It will take a while to complete our investigation. To determine if you were the prey of the deceased, or they were yours. Or if the whole lot of you were in cahoots." He sits back, baring his teeth.

Another policeman brings the detective a sheet of paper that looks like it's been torn from a school exercise book. He whispers something in the detective's ear, placing the sheet before him. The detective studies it for a few moments. Then he sits forward again, looking at Daniel as if an overhead light has suddenly been switched on, as if seeing him for the first time. The detective takes up the paper, holds it aloft. Triumphantly, as if about to deliver a coup de grace. Daniel looks at the childish handwriting on it. "In this document the deceased stipulate what must be done with their effects. Everything is left to you. *Everything*. It's not a valid will. And as a potential suspect you will provisionally not be entitled to anything. But: It casts a different light on your involvement." The policeman lights a cigarette, inhales strongly, stroking his shaved head. "A *completely* different light."

This performance is now starting to bore Daniel. His thoughts leapfrog to South Africa. The last time he was in Cape Town was before meeting the Serbs. He thinks of his sister, trapped in her unblemished life behind electrified fences. Of his father, blissfully unaware of almost all aspects of his son's existence. He tries to remember fragments of conversation with either of them during that last visit, just a sentence they might have exchanged. He cannot come up with anything.

His thoughts drift to his laptop computer in the rucksack by his feet. He lowers his hand, stroking the rectangle of the device through the canvas. He thinks of the cool aluminium casing housing the electronics, of the near-silent keyboard. His fingers are itching. It's time to return to his usual life. To re-establish order.

Daniel raises his arms, lacing his fingers behind his head. He smiles. As he and the policeman face each other, neither blinking, he wonders if he would be able to return to that flat on the outskirts of Belgrade. What might be there of interest to him? Perhaps he should go through Oliver's pile of DVDs and select a few. Perhaps there's something truly rare, something hard to find. But who still needs DVDs? You can get everything in digital format these days. He must get himself one of those tiny projectors like Oliver had, that you can connect to an iPhone.

Daniel slides down onto his coccyx, his hands still behind his head. No, he decides, from here he'll go straight to the airport, take a flight to London. And he will resolve never again to lose himself in some random former Eastern Block city.

The policeman lifts an open hand and brings it down hard

on the desk. With the other hand he reaches for a thin file. Plucking out a photo, he dangles it in front of Daniel: an image of two bodies suspended from the ceiling. Oliver and Yugo. Or the empty shells that used to bear those names. The detective raises his voice, asks a brusque question.

He watches Daniel intently while the interpreter translates: "You tell me: Why did they have to die?"

Daniel drops his hands into his lap, leans forward: "They died, sergeant—or captain or colonel, whatever you are—to liberate me. Like Jesus they died for me."

Daniel settles back in his chair, looking into the policeman's eyes as the interpreter translates. The man's air of authority shrivels instantly. He is no longer convinced by his own performance. He avoids eye contact, turns the photo upside-down on the desk. He swivels in his chair, mutters something dismissive in Serbian. Something, if Daniel were to guess, like: "Just get him out of my sight." Or: "I know he was involved, this bloody slippery Brit. But I have no grounds to detain him."

The interpreter does not translate. Taking Daniel's arm, she lifts him to his feet. Daniel looks at her in surprise. Not just an interpreter, but a handler as well. She leads him out.

And there, in the waiting room, she is sitting: Oliver's mother. Daniel meets her gaze. Her eyes are red with weeping, mascara is smeared over her cheek. When she sees Daniel, she jumps up and starts shouting. She points at him, her voice raw. If Daniel were once again to surmise-translate, it would be something like: "They were your prey! You devoured them! Left nothing of them behind!" She doesn't stop, words keep coming. Something, perhaps, like: "A curse on you. And on your sons, and their sons!" (or maybe: "On your father, and his father!") Then she charges at him. The interpreter lets go of Daniel, puts herself between him and the mother, grabs her, embraces her, roughly comforts her, restrains her. The woman's arms flail over the interpreter's shoulders towards Daniel, wilder and wilder. The talons of a mother wolf, claws that would rend Daniel to pieces in the blink of an eye.

Daniel looks through the taxi window at the outskirts of Belgrade, lowers the window to let the breeze onto his face. He inhales, deeply and with pleasure. The air smells of something he has trouble placing: ash or iron. He takes out his mobile phone, messages Mirko, arranges to meet him the next day for lunch in Soho. He won't breathe a word to his friend about the last week. He takes the laptop from his rucksack, flips it open. The battery is almost fully charged and it's half an hour's drive to the airport. He starts typing frantically, a black torrent of words. Unfamiliar words, conjuring up lives with no link to his.

When he blinks, only slightly more slowly than usual, he briefly glimpses two bodies hanging against the light. Thus, he thinks, is fever stoked. Thus is one aroused from death.

2. Lost in Malaysia

Daniel tends to avoid the southern suburbs of the city. To his mind, everything there is dank and mouldy. In the last few months, though, he's had to spend many days and nights in Constantia, assisting his father in his decline. It started abruptly, the deterioration: There was a fall, an operation, a memory apparently wiped clean overnight, a visit to a neurologist, an image on a scan of atrophy in the parts of the brain that govern memory and spatial orientation.

The last time Daniel spoke to his sister, she said: "Why don't you go and live with him? You have the freedom and the flexibility, don't you?" Which is to say: *Unlike me, with my sacred duty as wife and mother to succour my blonde children and my surgeon husband—the guarantor of my custom-tailored existence—you have no obligation to anybody. Now do what you have to, you who have begotten no offspring, who have neither real profession nor spouse, who owe your free-wheeling lifestyle to your father's finances. Our debilitated father is yours till he dies.* His sister lives with her husband in a residential estate outside Paarl, a place with huddled houses, man-made ponds, a polo field, a distant view of mountains and the silence of a psychiatric ward. She is also blonde, his sister. Her teeth are whiter than clouds.

He locks up the house that his father will never see again. The place, spacious enough to house three families, these days bears the scars of inadequate maintenance: a gutter coming unstuck, weeds forging their way through paving. That's how it will have to remain until the estate has been administered and every tangible asset, or those manifesting as entries in the databases of investment firms, has been liquidated. And if somebody wants to force a window to bed down in the sitting room or have a morning bath in the swimming pool, nobody will stop them.

Daniel hesitates, turns back. He unlocks the front door again, leaves it like that.

They follow the mountain's sinuosities to the city. Daniel drives much too fast. His father lies back; below them the buildings and harbour dissolve in a wash of light. At his apartment block in Tamboerskloof he drives into the garage. Mercifully, there is a lift, and even though his father digs his fingers into Daniel's upper arm, he is able to walk on his own. He settles his father in the second bedroom, with its view of Lion's Head. He unpacks the suitcase that he packed for his father twenty minutes ago on the other side of the mountain. Enough to last him from laundry day to laundry day, and to the end of his days: seven pairs of socks, seven pairs of underpants, seven handkerchiefs, seven pairs of trousers, seven shirts. A jersey and a jacket. One pair of shoes.

So now his father is living with him, here against this slope overlooking the city. And in this bedroom is the last mattress that he will ever sleep on, surely, the last wardrobe door he'll open, the last bedside lamp that he'll switch on.

Their routine starts to take shape, with few variations. His father generally wakes up early, takes a seat at the kitchen table, waits for breakfast cereal. Patiently. In the early stages of his dementia diagnosis, and when he started taking his neurological medication, he was racked with anxiety. He was seized with a great sense of urgency: By means of endless lists, their items systematically crossed out, he tried to order the disordered catalogue of consciousness, tried to reprogramme the corrupt databases. He started phoning Daniel, with whom he would normally have spoken at most twice or three times a year, a dozen times a day to ask the same questions—about his investments, his bank accounts, the service intervals of his car (which he no longer drove), his doctor's appointments. Questions that Daniel could only start answering once he'd brought himself up to date on his father's affairs and taken charge of them. But now his father is meekly eating cornflakes with milk, maybe a banana, perhaps some tea. Shortly after breakfast he wants to go out, sit down somewhere for coffee. Then they return so that he can have his rest. Sometimes they vary the routine, have breakfast somewhere else. Lunch is generally at home. And after lunch they wait (in vain) for the heat to abate, take another walk, once again find coffee somewhere.

They have their morning coffee while the rest of the city is gearing up: In tower blocks, magnetic strips are swiped to slide open office doors, computers are zoomed into life, faces are turned towards air conditioners. His father says nothing, drinks his coffee. Their time together is marked by boundless silences. There is a veil of fog separating his father from the world, and the two of them from each other. When Daniel asks his father how he's feeling, he first has to reflect for a long time, then points vaguely at his forehead, mutters something about pressure, about rain clouds, about dusk. Even though the sky above is deep blue.

Back in the flat, Daniel plays music for his father. Every day he wants to listen to the same playlist—baroque favourites. Daniel streams it on his TV—a sophisticated device that somebody set up for him, with a small sub-device synchronised with his iPhone. He controls the music from his phone, making the items play in random order. He sits down at the dining-room table without looking at his father on the couch. He flips open his computer, tries to write. The atmosphere in here is stale, and the stuffiness isn't expelled when the balcony doors are thrown open. Every time Daniel arrives in Cape Town, he opens everything up, airing the place, but a sense of absence keeps lingering. It's as if they're sitting in a room that no-one has entered in decades.

On a Monday, shortly after lunch—bread and fruit, which his father hardly touched—they take another walk in the heat hanging motionless over the city bowl. They stop for coffee as usual. When they're seated, facing each other, his father grows apologetic, as if feeling compelled to initiate a modicum of interaction. "I'm sorry I'm such bad company," he says. "I really don't want to be a burden to my children in my old age."

"It's nothing," Daniel hears himself say. "And it's no burden. All that's important is that we're here together." In fact, he wants to get up and walk away, abandon his father here. Not go back to the flat, but take a short cut up Signal Hill, past Lion's Head, up Table Mountain. As far as he can go. Without looking back once at the lone figure seated down there at the table for two.

Without planning to do so, he starts telling his father about one of his exes in London. Even though his father still recognises his children, there's hardly a trace of memory left. Admittedly, what his father would previously have known about Daniel doesn't amount to much; there was very little information there to shrivel away with the cerebral tissue. For at least a dozen years, they've never discussed a single aspect of each other's personal lives. His father would have known that Daniel was commuting at irregular intervals between London and Cape Town, that he sometimes penned bits of political and cultural journalism for British and South African newspapers, that he wrote fiction in the intervals. A peculiar pastime in the eyes of someone like his father the investment banker, who had spent his prior working life in the world of financial power brokering. Years ago, when his father's approval still counted for something, Daniel worked as a management consultant in London. Of the shape of the life he's leading these days, his father would not have an inkling. Especially not his personal life.

What Daniel recounts now, he does because he knows his father will have forgotten it within an hour or two. Or maybe a minute or two. And perhaps also to break the silence. It's a fragment of the story of an old relationship. "I must tell you about Eamon, Dad. One of my ex-lovers up there in the North. An Irishman. Four years ago he moved in with me in London, and about eleven months later moved back to Dublin." His father just smiles.

Daniel delves into the details of a trip he took with Eamon. Why he's selected this particular fragment, he can't say. He talks about their week in eastern Ireland, where Eamon grew up. As he describes the Irish landscapes in detail, he observes his father's frozen smile and blurred eyes. Then he describes his and Eamon's mornings in a poky guesthouse, adorned with Irish kitsch for the streams of American tourists travelling there to find their roots. He looks straight at his father while expanding on the almost unbearable delight he and Eamon took in each other's bodies in the mornings, there amidst shamrocks and grinning green leprechauns, while the sun rose over the Irish Sea.

Daniel stops talking, tries to read his father's eyes. He wants to retrieve a scene from his childhood: one of him and his father together, just the two of them. Father and son kicking a ball, son on father's shoulders in a swimming pool, laughter and play-wrestling on a lawn at dusk. But the gaze is empty. All Daniel's mind's eye can come up with—whether he's conjuring or remembering it is unclear—is a snapshot of his father and him somewhere on a wintry beach. Perhaps in Cape Town, perhaps on a European trip. Both of them silent in the wind. Daniel intently watching his dad. The father putting his hands in his pockets, the son instantly copying him . . .

The image dissipates as quickly as it came to him. He regards the passive figure facing him, the vacuous smile. He wants to grab hold of his father and shake him, shock his brain into action.

Today his father rests after lunch instead of going for a walk. The heat keeps getting fiercer: A protracted heat wave is predicted. Daniel stands in the passage, where it's coolest. He looks at the laptop on the dining table, at the sleeping screen. The old resistance must be overcome. He can't evade it, must immerse himself in the discomfort. He must make his peace with the inexorability of that which must be written, with its unbearable incompleteness. The importunity of stories, Daniel thinks—this *urge*—will one day be his downfall.

Sometimes, in the evenings, his father has a surprisingly lucid interval. It comes an hour or so after taking his medication, including a potent sleeping pill that's supposed to knock him out. The first time it happens it is a shock to Daniel. It's as if a ghost from the past is visiting him, here above the shimmering city and bay. His father is in bed already, but suddenly wants to *talk*. He is full of life and gestures. He makes recommendations about the management of his assets, utters insights into recent political events—evidently he does absorb facts while paging, apparently unseeing, through newspapers in the morning. Somewhere information is temporarily stored, until a curtain opens a chink and the brain can process it. And he discourses on the past, on aspects of his own life that mainly exclude Daniel, such as his professional life and travels; or, in a gentler voice, on Daniel's late mother. Then also on his grandchildren, the surgeon's wellfed spawn somewhere near Paarl. He doesn't mention, as must surely come home to him in these moments, that he hasn't seen these children, or his daughter, in months.

At such times Daniel is struck dumb, his throat constricted. Is this his father of two decades ago being resurrected here before him? Or of six months ago? It unnerves him, this indeterminacy. Who is the man in this bed? Daniel feels as if anything he might bring himself to say in these moments would be a secret betrayed, as if it could all be held against him. Experiencing a kind of shame, he guards every word. His father steams ahead, unburdens his heart—cognitively and emotionally he is suddenly *present*, intellectually primed. Again some former self. With abhorrence, Daniel regards the man hoisting himself further and further off the pillows, higher and higher against the headboard as his confidence burgeons. He registers his father's own amazement at the clear stream of water rinsing his thoughts, at the sunlight penetrating where for a long time the sun has not shone.

"Go to sleep now, Dad, you had your sleeping pill ages ago."

There is even a glimmer of humour: "You just want to get rid of me, don't you? Now that we can talk face to face at last." His father regards him with a knowing smile. You'd think it was all a show, the day's disorientation. That this is his true father, devoting what remains of his life to playing a tedious trick on his recalcitrant son. Teaching him a lesson.

There he sits, the old man: He gesticulates while talking, his voice excited, his sentences complete, his face animated.

But when his father appears in the kitchen the next morning in a state of confusion, the morning sun in his tousled hair, and asks, "Where are we now?" as he searches through rooms he's convinced he's never seen before, Daniel knows that this bewilderment cannot possibly be an affectation.

They're in a dreary breakfast spot on the lower slopes of Signal Hill. His father says nothing, just sits, now and again touching his head. He's not totally absent: When Daniel speaks, he smiles, says something polite and vacuous in response. Daniel inspects his father's face. How do you make sense of the uneven course of the mind's emptying, the way you can at no time judge with accuracy what's being taken in or processed?

The dimmer his father's presence, and the vaguer his smile, the more freely Daniel can talk. He elaborates on his series of failed relationships in London. The accounts become more and more intimate. *It's your fault!* he wants to excoriate his father—right after dwelling in detail on the Brit who also lived with him for a while. Josh: an architect, slightly built, Jewish, a decade younger than Daniel. One evening after an argument, Josh shook his head and said: "What's wrong with you isn't something I—and I dare say anyone—can fix." Then he walked out of the front door and never returned.

When his father says nothing, Daniel continues with another one—the German with the tattoos on his hands and neck. "You wouldn't have approved of him, Dad, that lover of mine. He worked as a ticket seller at the National Portrait Gallery. Udo was his name. I don't exactly know what went wrong there. When I think back to him, then I remember our long weekend away in Devon. We went for a walk in a light spring shower. In a field blue with crocuses and bluebells. We stood under some birch trees, chest to chest, and locked our hands around each other's wrists. I thought, this is something, or the beginning of something. A powerful current flowed between us. I could feel it. In my blood. And then, after the weekend, I never heard a word from him again."

He looks into his father's eyes, trying to find something. "No, wait, Dad, let me amend my previous statement. There is *no* lover that you would have approved of."

His father makes a face, touches his forehead. "There's so much pressure here," he says. "As if my head's about to explode."

This time he's made his father walk a long way. They're sitting in a coffee shop in lower Higgovale.

"Tell me news about yourself." His father smiles while talking—encouraging, kindly, replete with incomprehension. "How are you getting on, for instance, with your writing?"

Daniel is taken aback. First because his father has remembered that he writes, but even more because he's asking Daniel about it—for the first time ever. Now that the synaptic sparks are misfiring so fitfully.

Daniel ignores the question. He starts telling another London tale, of the two Serbs he befriended a year or so ago. How he met them—Oliver and Yugo—at a retrospective of Agnes Martin, the American minimalist. How they became friends, how they moved in with him in his flat in Borough.

His father's smile vanishes. "That is a different story," he says, shaking his head. "Not the one I want to hear."

"Perhaps, yes," says Daniel. "But I want to force it in here. Or rather, it insists on forming part of our conversation." The more his father forgets, the more Daniel wants to remember. And he wants to make his father know that he remembers.

His father gets to his feet abruptly, starts tottering away. Daniel pays the bill, follows.

Early evening, dusk. The moon rises, a sluggish, gravid ball. Behind Daniel the baroque music is playing for his father, who's on the couch with his head thrown back, only half alive.

Daniel leans over the balcony's glass balustrade. His life—so delicately balanced between two countries—makes it possible to approach South Africa as a stranger, he thinks. No, as somebody from another planet. That's the way the Brits like it: to observe everything as if from a spaceship. He can write and expound on the politics here, stay attuned to its finest nuance, but he need never get close to it. That's what the lights look like tonight, like something contemplated from a great distance. And yet, should he extend an arm, he could touch the face of the city with his fingertips. He keeps his hands in his pockets.

His father wakes, comes out onto the balcony. He doesn't gaze out over the wide expanse of lights, but up at the neomodernist cubes against Signal Hill.

"The language of rain," his father says.

Daniel sniffs the air. It's warm and bone dry. His father turns, facing the city's silver glow. "Look at the glittering landscape of glass," he says. "The evening is upon us."

Indeed, Daniel thinks, here it is—the respite of darkness, in this town that he finds so depressing. So over-illuminated, so overwhelmed with sun: city of guileless, languid joys, of cocktails and damp swimming trunks, of joggers on mountainsides.

The music still playing indoors spreads a suave sheet over the buildings beneath them. Daniel closes his eyes, tuning in to the dusk, to the soothing undertone of seaweed in the whiff of night. Beneath his feet the balcony floor is still lukewarm. When he opens his eyes, his father has sat down inside once more. Daniel sits down next to him, the balcony door still ajar. The TV screensaver is showing cities seen from above while the baroque music plays on: At the moment it's Los Angeles, city of angels, gliding past ceremonially. A nub of freeways, processions of cars in slow motion.

He thinks of a pop video he once saw, featuring Los Angeles as a future city. The actual city, recognisable, but with futuristic buildings added here and there. A smear of luminosity, of aluminium and glass. Lights flickering faintly in the haze.

"Where are we now?" his father demands loudly.

"My flat." Daniel speaks softly. The screensaver has segued to Dubai's desert towers with their rooftop swimming pools. An ex of Daniel's who'd lived in Dubai for a while once told him that the desert air warmed the swimming pools so much that the water had to be cooled electrically to refresh swimmers. Another story for a coffee session, the one about the Dubai ex.

"Yes, but which country?"

"It doesn't matter, Dad. This country, that country . . . Or rather, your instinct is spot-on. Here is as good as nowhere. For you, but also for me." Daniel grins. "That's the one thing we have in common." Here they are, stranded together on their elevated platform, above the cool shimmer of an amorphous city.

Daniel thinks about his conversation with the neurologist about the startlingly lucid intervals his father sometimes experiences. (He didn't add that the lucid father is more of a stranger than the befuddled one.) The doctor was sceptical. Whatever the case, tonight is not one of those nights. His father is amiably obtuse, his face adorned with a feeble-minded smirk. On the TV screen, the all-seeing camera now approaches Hong Kong's glittering spires from on high.

Daniel gives his father his medicine, withdraws to his own room. He switches on the ceiling fan, lies down naked on his back. He dozes off as if slipping into one of Dubai's chilled rooftop swimming pools.

The pressure in his father's head intensifies. Exponentially, it seems to Daniel, an unsettling progression. And he eats less and less, baby food by now: mashed banana, yoghurt, pawpaw, oatmeal porridge, rooibos tea with honey. On the news his father watches an item about a train conductor in Kalk Bay who was stabbed in the head with a knife by a passenger. His father's hands involuntarily find his own head. "I could swear," he declares, "I have a blade in my skull."

Once again Daniel takes his father to the neurologist, who speculates that, apart from atrophy, there may also be a build-up of fluid in the brain. They do balance tests—make him stand with eyes closed, push him to see if he falls, catch him when it happens. They also do a memory test. One aspect of this involves reading his father a random name and address to repeat ten minutes later. Harry Barnes, 10 Orchards Close, Kingsbridge, Devon. (It must be a British test.) When the occupational therapist asks his father, after a series of other tests, to recall the address, he looks at Daniel forlornly. He could whisper something, relieve his father's bewilderment and humiliation. His father's gaze becomes a plea; Daniel's lips remain sealed.

Back home, they lapse more or less into the familiar routine. On the TV, while Dido's lament from Purcell's opera is playing, the screensaver once again shows aerial views of cities. Hong Kong reflected in its own black bay, Dubai's glass towers with their sky-high swimming pools.

They find themselves in the late afternoon in a coffee shop, high up in one of Tamboerskloof's quaint Victorian streets. There is nothing, Daniel thinks, that he cannot tell his father. All obstacles have been dispelled. The psychic space between the two of them is like a salt pan in a desert: white and flat and almost frictionless. Still, Daniel does not utter a word today.

Teaspoons clink against saucers. His father points out birds pecking at crumbs on the pavement. On the way back his father is withdrawn, as if combatting the discomfort in his skull demands all his energy. He walks unseeing, two fingers to his temple, one foot in front of the other. Suddenly he stops and points at a power line. Dozens of pigeons are perched there. "Those are carrier pigeons," he says. "Who knows what planets they'll take their messages to."

Shortly after they reach home, an Egyptian goose skirls outside, one of a breeding pair that has settled in the swimming pool of the school across the road. His father perks up, hurries to the window, hypnotised by the birds down there. He seems to have eyes only for winged creatures now, big and small. He looks up, slits his eyes, scans the sky in vain for flocks.

The neurologist books Daniel's father for a lumbar puncture. He is admitted to a formerly Catholic hospital in the southern suburbs. There are still empty niches here and there where effigies of the Madonna must have stood, a cross is hewn in stone above an entrance and the wards still bear the names of saints. But the habits of nursing nuns no longer swish down the corridors; the institution now belongs to one of the big hospital groups, has been corporately sterilised. Daniel sits reading next to his father's bed. They wait; the hours pass. The doctor is dealing with an emergency in intensive care, says the nurse. Daniel and his father are instructed to wait. And wait.

There is one other patient in the ward, a tall thin man with one bloodred eye. When Daniel sees him for the first time, it looks like an empty socket. Daniel quickly averts his gaze. When he glances back surreptitiously, he sees that the eyeball is there after all, just severely bloodshot.

They come to collect his father for an electroencephalogram. The technician drapes electrodes over his father's head, works the wires into a node over his forehead. The wires trail from the back of his head like seaweed. On the technician's screen, graph lines throb in febrile patterns. Now and then there's a sudden simultaneous trough in the striations. The technician frowns. "I'm getting such a lot of artefact today along with the impedance," she says, as if Daniel is supposed to understand what she means.

His father turns his head, points at the screen. "Does it measure the flight of electric birds? Of robot flocks?" A handful of the electrodes drop off. The technician shakes her head, replaces his arm on the bed, tells him to lie still. She gets up and repositions the electrodes, repeats her measurements.

All the electrodes are removed. His father is returned to the ward. The patient with the blood-red eye has constant visitors—an endless rotation of physiotherapists, occupational therapists, neurologists, ophthalmologists. Each is treated to the poor man's story. He is a commercial pilot. Six weeks ago he was in Malaysia for a few days, where he was attacked in the street and left for dead. A Good Samaritan took him to hospital. He was unconscious for three days. He had broken bones in his face, cuts and bruises everywhere, as well as cerebral haemorrhage. He remembers nothing of the incident, and only part of the weeks-long stay in hospital afterwards. What he remembers most clearly, he says, is the patient file that read, where his name should have been: *Unknown*. He's only just been transferred to South Africa.

His flying licence was automatically suspended on account of his injuries and now he has to try to get it back. Hence all the tests. The therapists and specialists keep circling, each with their own test or examination. Each with a file or clipboard in hand. Frequently the curtain around the bed is drawn, according to a slightly varying ritual. Time and again the story is repeated, each time with the memory lapse at the centre. The same occupational therapist who assisted Daniel's father comes to administer a cognitive and memory test on the former pilot, asks the same questions.

His father lies with closed eyes; Daniel mutters the answers under his breath: a list of words starting with "p" ("peacock, pink, pad"), nouns to repeat ("lemon, table, ball"), the address of the Brit in Devon that has to be regurgitated at the end of the test. The man with the red eye gets few of the answers right, remembers hardly anything. Daniel has to bite his tongue.

"*He's* not going to fly again," Daniel's father announces loudly, without opening his eyes. Daniel is startled. He'd been under the impression that his father was asleep, or at least dozing. For a few moments there is shocked silence from behind the curtain before the occupational therapist hesitantly proceeds with the test. The ex-pilot now speaks more softly; his answers are even more desperate.

The neurologist at last pays a late-night visit to his father's bed. He makes the octogenarian curl up, knees drawn up, reduced to a foetus. Then the doctor pushes a thick needle into his lower back. The cerebral fluid surges up into a pipette; the meniscus indicates pressure. The doctor drains off several vials.

"Nice and clear," the doctor says. "A good sign."

Daniel drives home, goes to bed in his flat on the other

side of the mountain. He considers letting his sister know, in her soundless white house near Paarl, that their father is in hospital. No, he thinks, he won't disturb her. Such a brittle existence, one so effectively excluding the world of raw experience, should not be unsettled. His sister would certainly prefer their father simply to evanesce, to vanish into the ether without this bothersome process of corporeal dissolution. She sees to it, in any case, that she does not have to witness the disintegration. Let them rest, Daniel decides, his sister and her husband, there by Paarl. Let the mountain breezes breathe fresh air over her and her husband's sleeping bodies.

The following morning there are two visitors for the ex-pilot whose life was destroyed one evening in the Far East. His parents, apparently. They draw the curtain around his bed. Daniel is sitting next to his own father's bed, a book in hand, but he can't help listening to the muffled voices. Nurses are chattering in the corridor. Cleaners laugh somewhere. He overhears only floating fragments of the conversation.

" . . . how they found you in the hospital . . . three weeks after the attack . . . " says the pilot's mother.

"I only remember from about week four or so," says the pilot. A sentence or two is lost in the hubbub.

Scraps of the maternal voice: "Nothing on Facebook. It was . . . She told us there was a website. It was only when we posted a message and your photo . . . We couldn't believe it . . . Then we contacted the airline . . . They went to your hotel, just your toothbrush lying there, your pilot uniform. Neatly laid out for your flight back . . . a pair of clean socks." She is sobbing now.

"Which website?"

A cleaner laughs uproariously in the corridor; a sister (perhaps one of the last remaining nuns?) silences her.

"Lostinmalaysia.com," says the pilot's mother, " . . . went through the list of names . . . without it we might still have been looking. Nobody could get a name or address from you . . . And at last, at last, they found you there: in a white bed in a hospital in Malaysia." The nurses and cleaners are silent now, as if listening. "With three broken bones in your face and bleeding on your brain." The woman sobs when she says "brain."

"But now," declares the pilot, "everything is fine again. Just the last few tests. And then I want to see Emma and the children. When are they coming?"

Daniel's father wants to get up and take a walk in the hospital gardens. Daniel holds his arm to steady him, goes along to prevent him getting lost somewhere among the shrubs. As they're walking, Daniel wonders: why "lostinmalaysia.com" rather than "missinginmalaysia.com"? As if wanting to signal something alluring, something bleakly romantic.

As his father sits down on a bench and looks up, he says: "Where are they? I can *feel* the wings."

When Daniel walks down the long corridor with his father, back to the ward, the pilot's parents are there, leaning against a wall, whispering.

"And how would that help him?" the mother says. "What do you want me to tell him? That she hasn't wanted to see him for over a decade, and now less than ever? And, worse, that the children *were* here, even though he doesn't know it, and they don't want to come again . . . ?"

It's the fourth morning since Daniel's father's discharge from the hospital. Last night he had one of his bouts of clarity, accompanied by free-flowing conversation, or at least a monologue. He sat on the balcony talking about stock markets; remarking, as an aside, that the flat was too crowded for two people. He wanted to know whether the house in Constantia had been sold. The house that was too extravagant for Daniel's tight-fisted, spartan father, and which he bought just because his wife wanted it. It was sold a long time ago, Daniel lied, and wondered whether a colony of homeless people had already made themselves at home in the spacious lounge, or were taking the opportunity to cool down in the pool before it turns green and slimy.

This morning his father is looking ashen, his skin drawn tightly over the cheekbones. The tapping of the brain fluid has brought no noticeable relief. They're sitting in a café in lower Tamboerskloof. Coffee once again. And, again, a plate of food that his father hardly touches. He's had nothing but a few mouthfuls of water today.

When they get home, Daniel leaves soft fruit out on the kitchen counter where it's visible, as if for a shy bird, in case his father does, after all, want something to eat. The baroque list is playing again. The more Daniel listens to it, the stranger it sounds. Like music he has never heard before. He has to look at the playlist to confirm that it is indeed what they've been listening to over the last few weeks. It is, the pieces haven't changed. And yet, somehow they've been recomposed; the zeroes and ones of the data on the hard drive have been reshuffled to become something that is cooler on the ear, like raindrops on parched lips.

The next day over coffee Daniel's father enquires about his daughter. "Have you heard from her recently, Daniel?" It's clear that, despite his inability to form new memories, he's somehow registered or sensed that she's stopped visiting him. That she hasn't called, that he hasn't seen his grandchildren in a long time.

"My sister with her joyless smile has forsaken you, Dad. You will never again hold her pearly hand in yours." Daniel's voice is cruel. Let the truth chart new paths in his father's brain, he thinks. Then he immediately starts telling his father about the Serbs again; he can't stop himself. How they returned to Belgrade, how he went on holiday with them in Southern Germany, where they stayed in a town where three rivers converge. He recounts how he had a relationship of sorts with each of the two Serbs, and with the two of them together. What a relief, Daniel thinks, to be telling the story to someone who is under no pressure to attach any meaning to it.

He wants to push through the tale of the Serbs, even though his father has no interest in it, even though it has hardly any link to his father's own story playing out here on Cape Town's slopes. And even though his father is becoming increasingly pale and distracted.

But Daniel does, after all, relent. He leaves the end of the story for their next coffee or breakfast. "Tomorrow," he says, "I'll tell you the rest."

"I know how that story goes, Daniel." His father frowns. "What I want to hear more about is my daughter."

"I'm sure you'll soon hear from her directly," Daniel says curtly. "And that she'll bring the children for a visit." His nephew and niece, Daniel suddenly realises, have never visited this flat in all the years he's had it.

When they walk back, Daniel's father's clutching fingers cut into his arm. All his father's wanted to do since his return from hospital is go for walks. When they head up the steeper streets, his father sometimes has to stop to catch his breath, but he's stronger than his frail-looking body suggests. Perhaps, Daniel thinks, it is *he* who's being dragged up the cruel slopes, perhaps the 82-year-old's hands are steering *him*. As the brain implodes, the body is apparently secretly becoming fitter. Younger even.

At home, Daniel sits down in front of his computer, hands on the keyboard. He types a sentence, erases it. It's too hot to work. He lies down on his bed, falls asleep beneath the ceiling fan's lazy rotations. When he wakes up, his father is standing at the dining table. From his computer screen, near his father's elbow, a blue glow emanates. An internal fan is whirring at high speed, cooling the machine. Somehow the computer has been woken from its slumber. A moth's wing against the screen? Can heat or sharp light revive a computer? Or is it possible that his father was fiddling with the keyboard, that he's been reading what Daniel's writing?

Daniel walks over to the computer, stands next to his father. His unfinished piece is displayed on the screen, the working title, *[Where the Wolves Mate]*, at the top. Before Daniel went for a nap, he'd been working on the ending, he's sure of that. Now the document is open on the first page.

His father drops his head into his hand. "It's unbearable," he says. "As if my skull is being clenched in a vice."

Can his father even read with comprehension any longer? The neurologist had explained that constructing textual meaning would become increasingly problematic. His father is simply unable to integrate a new paragraph with what has gone before, because, by then, the previous paragraphs have already been forgotten.

Daniel closes the screen. "Dad, I was really hoping the discomfort in your head would have subsided by now, that you'd be better." He's trying to contain the impatience in his voice. "Every test has been run. There is no infection, no tumour or growth. And if there were increased pressure, then the draining of excess fluid would have lowered it." He shakes his head. "The neurologist has no further advice, no other explanation."

His father looks at him, smiles brightly at his son's

frustration with the disintegrating paternal body. "Not everything that happens in the human brain can be measured and tested by doctors."

An aeroplane becomes vaguely audible outside. Daniel's father hurries out to the balcony, looks up. "He's flying again!" he shouts. "That man from Malaysia."

Daniel follows his father outside, looks up at the gleaming craft, at the dissipating line of smoke trailing it. There's more than one plane in the world, he wants to tell his father, and not just one pilot. And the man you're thinking of isn't even from Malaysia.

His father keeps gazing up, as if searching for the gleaming trajectories of interplanetary carrier pigeons. Then he goes inside, sits down on the couch, tilts his head backwards, closes his eyes. He grows even paler, if that is possible. Daniel stays on the balcony, thinking of the poor pilot, who is probably still waiting in vain in hospital. Waiting for his wife and children, and for someone to sign off on his health, to discharge him. For the panels of experts to declare his body and brain fit. To confirm that he may once again fly a plane freighted with sleeping bodies over expansive night cities. Without sucking flocks of birds into the engines, without letting the steel hull tumble earthwards through layers of light and shade. Without making bodies and steel and concrete disappear in a cloud of kerosene.

Heat collects in the city bowl, radiating from buildings and streets. The forecast for today is 36 degrees Celsius, but in the glow of the mountain it feels even hotter. As usual, Daniel's father wants to go for a walk.

Concrete seethes soundlessly; the tar is melting. Daniel looks down at the parched city, thinks of the empty dams and reservoirs in the region. Of the water that will run out in a month or two, taps that will run dry, pipes that will crumble. He likes the idea of this stuffy hollow as a desert in the making. He takes his father higher and higher up Signal Hill. When they reach the topmost street, his father objects. He shakes his head, looking at the steep curve of the tar, it's too much for him.

Daniel takes his arm. "You're the one who wanted to walk. I know it's hot, but it's good for you to stay fit."

He waits for his father to complain. The old man says nothing, just puts one foot in front of the other, more hesitant than before. Daniel feels his fingers cutting into his father's arm. He pulls his father up the hill. He thinks about how, over the course of his father's entire life of normal brain function, he never let his son finish a single sentence without interrupting him. How is he now so tongueless? With his free hand, his father touches his own skull, making a barely audible sound of distress.

"Perhaps," Daniel says, "your head is boiling. Maybe your brain is cooking in its own sauce." His father still doesn't say anything, just looks up at the scorched fynbos further up the hill. Daniel regrets his words. He looks down at the city, which is dissolving in white heat. How long before his father no longer even knows who this tormenting younger man is?

They walk all the way to the end, where the street abruptly ends in a cul-de-sac. Then all the way back down. His father isn't up to having coffee. His face is crimson, he insists on going back to the flat. When they get there, he goes straight to his room to lie down.

A few hours later, in the hot early evening, Daniel goes to his father's bed. He's still asleep. Daniel rests his hand on his father's forehead. It burns his palm. Suddenly his father makes a snorting sound and moves, says something like:

"We'll make cities tumble. This is the end of music." Daniel quickly backs into the passage, closes the door despite knowing that it will make it even hotter in there. The building is like a feverish animal.

When suppertime arrives, his father is still asleep. Daniel doesn't wake him—he won't, after all, eat anything. And, if Daniel is honest, he's relieved to be spending an evening without the baroque favourites, and without the deceptive calm of cities and highways gliding past on the TV screen. He certainly isn't up to one of his father's unnerving intervals of clarity either.

He isn't hungry. He opens the fridge, closes it again, goes to bed early.

When Daniel wakes under the sluggish blades of the ceiling fan, in the bright morning light, it is almost nine. He gets up, listens at his father's door. Nothing—he's still asleep. Daniel sits down at the dining table, presses a key on the keyboard to wake up the computer. He reads through the chaotic draft of *[Where the Wolves Mate]*. He deletes a few things here and there, changes the order of a sentence or two. He is constantly distracted by flies that are so dazed by the heat you can squash them under your thumb. He doesn't formulate a single new sentence.

He gets up, knocks on his father's door. No reaction. He opens it and walks in. His father is lying with his head back and his mouth open. Daniel approaches. He bends forward, listening with his ear close to his father's nose, puts his hand on the heart, feels the pulse. He does these things with the grave air of a doctor. The heart is no longer beating. His father's body is cold, the wrist in Daniel's hand already stiff.

Daniel sits down in the lounge, aware of his own breathing. He listens for a noise from his father's room, even though he knows there won't be any. He goes back to the room, switches on his father's electric razor. It sounds loud and rude. Then he shaves his father's face. He moves the chin back and forth with two fingers while guiding the little machine, first one cheek, then the neck and chin, then the other cheek. The skin is cool to the touch. He is careful and thorough. The razor obediently follows the contours of his father's face. He pulls the sheet neatly over his father's chest, up to his chin. He opens the blind so that the light pours in and Lion's Head is visible from the bed.

He goes out, locks the front door. He takes the lift down, fetches his sea kayak from the garage. For a moment he lingers in the cool space underneath the building, trying to banish the image of his father's body a few floors up. He ties the kayak to the roof of his car, drives out and down the street without looking back at his flat's windows.

He pushes the kayak into the water at Three Anchor Bay. He plans, for the first time in years, to row right across Table Bay, all the way to Milnerton. Water traffic has increased in the years since he last did this, he realises once he's passed Mouille Point: Multiple cargo ships are approaching him from the open sea, heavily loaded with multicoloured containers, heading into the harbour. When it looks like one will cross his path, Daniel estimates the vectors. He slows down, positions himself right in the path of the approaching ship. Then he waits. When it's almost too late, he begins rowing frantically to escape the approaching water turbulence and the threatening hull. Whoever is steering the ship would have no idea he is down here, and would, in any case, be unable to change course. The shadow passes over his flimsy boat. It's as if a towering building rises next to him; he can hear the water rumbling against the bow. His arms ache, his muscles burn. He is now rowing to escape the tonnes of steel, approaching relentlessly from barely twenty metres away. And then he's safe, back in the sun, where he can see black shapes flitting under the surface.

Over and over again he escapes the hulking shapes with seconds to spare. At Milnerton, he sits on the warm sand until his lungs stop burning. The sky is cobalt blue; sweat drips from his armpits. He looks at the vague profile of the mountain in the distance. Half an hour later he starts rowing back. He is still some distance from the ships' routes; for now he can relax. As he glides across the surface, he thinks of the view from his father's room, of the dozens of hikers' headlamps that will be flickering high up on Lion's Head tonight. And now his thoughts shift skywards. In his mind's eye, he can see a bird leaving its flock high above Cape Town, diving down to the window behind which his father's body lies. It wants to bring the old man a message, a small cylinder on its back containing a roll of parchment. On this is written *everything*. Everything the dead man's son has ever wanted to say to him. But the window is closed. And pecking against it won't help. Daniel suddenly realises: He never finished telling his father the story of the Serbs. Of little consequence now—no more than a placeholder for the rolled-up paragraphs nestling in the bird's back feathers.

Daniel closes his eyes as he rows, listening to the rhythm of the oars slapping the water. His mind moves on to the man with the brain injury, the one who disappeared in Malaysia for weeks. Daniel can see him in the cockpit of a jet, looking with astonishment at all the buttons and levers around him, all the gauges and lights, without having the vaguest idea what any of them do or measure. And now, with his eyes still closed, Daniel can see Table Bay from above, as if in an aerial photograph taken from a falling aircraft. A squadron of ships is approaching from the open sea. Between the ships and the harbour Daniel and his kayak are floating, a yellow speck on the wide expanse of water, lying there as clear and still as brain fluid.

*   *   *

The night after his father's death, Daniel is sitting in front of the TV in the living room as cities slide by on the screen. There is silence, the baroque soundtrack isn't playing. His arms are sore from all the rowing. The door of his father's room is closed, the body still in there. Daniel is listening to the city, at the sirens losing their urgency in the morning hours. He feels wide awake. But that cannot be, because he sees in front of him the back of a little boy walking into a cool forest, and it is him. It is evening, the tree trunks are basalt black. The child Daniel has a kind of wooden spool in his hand, on which is wound kilometres of thread. His father is present, outside the frame, holding one end of the thread. From somewhere a diffuse light is shining. The light and his father are one, his father's voice emanates from the light. The voice tells Daniel to keep walking, to let the thread unspool. "It doesn't matter how far you go, Daniel, I can follow the thread, I can feed it through my fingers the whole way. I'll always be able to find you at the other end." It is a voice Daniel hasn't heard since he was a child—full of mercy and hope for his son. But the boy is walking briskly, letting the gleaming thread unspool behind him like a spider's silk, and is already too far away to hear his dad.

When Daniel comes to in the Cape Town morning heat, he feels emptied out, as if he's been in a coma, or has amnesia. Then he is revisited by the last images of his dream. The boy is standing alone in the hazy forest. Daniel's dreaming self is now no longer looking from the outside at his childhood self—his perspective is also now that of the boy. When he looks down, he sees the wooden spool in his own hand. The thread has been completely unwound. And, when he looks around him, there is, as far as the eye can see, a rat's nest of thread, entangled with the trunks of a thousand trees— the result of days, or perhaps weeks or years, of walking in circles. In this vast light eclipsing spiderweb, Daniel has enmeshed himself.

He eats fruit for breakfast—fruit is all he'll have today. He waits a few hours, and at the height of the midday heat sends an email to his sister, informing her of their father's death. Then he starts to clean the kitchen, his and his father's dishes from the last few days. He straightens out the messy living room. It amazes him how today he handles every object (fork, plate, newspaper, spectacles) like a newborn thing. Everything is on the point of breaking; he must instruct everything in tenderness. And every single thing that touches his skin brings him pain.

He's just bitten into a peach in the kitchen, juice bleeding down his forearm, when his sister calls. She skips the niceties, wants to know when Daniel will be arranging the funeral.

"Our father wanted no funeral, no service or ceremony of any kind. He gifted his body to the university's medical faculty." As Daniel speaks into the cellphone, his voice full of authority, he opens the door to his father's room. He looks at the body under the sheet, at the rigid face, and continues: "They've already come to pick him up. He's lying in the anatomy department's dissection lab." On a stainless steel table, he wants to add. You could go and inspect him there if you wish, go and examine every square centimetre—the shoulders and ribs, the empty hands, the grieving scrotum—to satisfy yourself that he's really dead.

"I have a copy of the will," she says. "It says nothing about a funeral or the university." But he can already hear her tone changing from suspicion to relief.

"Our father wasn't one for wasting anything, you'll remember," Daniel says. "He wasn't in favour of excess. Or celebrations or rituals. He expressed his wishes quite clearly to me in his last days." Daniel knows he won't have to try too hard. His sister has already convinced herself. Christmas is in a few weeks and time is tight for a doctor's wife and mother. Now she'll be spared the drive to Cape Town, and a long afternoon away from home—just imagine the distance between church and graveyard, the hot, congested highways, the effort to arrange tea and refreshments! Now she won't have to miss her son's hockey match or her daughter's violin lesson. And her husband won't have to postpone a single operation.

She'll go and see their father's attorney about the estate, she says. She is appointed executor in the will; she presumes Daniel knows that. "Just email me the death certificate. I'm sure you understand that my children's financial needs, their futures, weigh heavily, and that things will have to be dealt with efficiently and—"

Daniel ends the call, switches off his phone. He goes out, sits down on the balcony. The heat has at last relented; the quality of the air is changing swiftly. He can't see it, but he knows that a cool cloud is starting to spill over the mountain. As the fog envelops the block of flats from behind and he waits for the city to disappear, a kind of calm that he hasn't experienced in decades descends on him. The fog brings with it an unworldly dusk. Beneath him the bay is still as flat as a sheet, but soon it will grow choppy, and a sea breeze will come and touch Daniel's cheeks. The tiniest droplets are starting to cling to his skin like a balm. He suddenly realises how thirsty he is. He sticks out his tongue, tastes the moist air.

He can't see his computer from here, but the screen must have lit up somehow—it's bathing the living room in the blue glow of an aquarium. By tomorrow, Daniel thinks, he will have forgotten every single detail of these last few weeks. He draws fog into his lungs and goes inside, where the keyboard awaits his damp fingers.

3.
HANKAI

Daniel had imagined that his father's will would, as in any number of films he'd seen, be read out loud in the attorney's office. That he and his sister would be present, hands anxiously clenched in their laps. Or no, wait—Daniel's brother-in-law would also be there, sitting next to her, his fingers intertwined with hers. He would dart the odd distrustful glance at Daniel, as if his wife had to be protected from her brother. (In what respect Daniel might menace her is not clear.) Then they'd listen to the bombastic reading, more aware of each other than of the attorney swivelling lazily in his chair, channelling their late father's wishes—or his bloody-mindedness. A subdued kind of séance. And then the dramatic surprise: Somebody would be cut off, would not inherit a cent.

Somebody? Well, it could only be Daniel. His sister's life choices, unlike his own, had met with his father's approval. She'd also (in a neat if blatant manoeuvre) made sure not to forget her father before he'd started forgetting everything and could no longer amend his will. Unlike Daniel, that is, who'd been forced to remember his father just as his father began to forget him.

While the lawyer paused between sentences, there'd be a general intake of breath. Then the lawyer would read the paragraph in which the testator explains why his assets should cross the generational boundaries so asymmetrically. A final moral lesson for the disadvantaged party: something to do with discipline and focus, with the qualities it behoves one to cultivate in order to lead a productive existence. All the characteristics that Daniel lacks. About how his sister had progeny whose interests should carry due weight, about how Daniel should now at last learn to earn an honest crust.

But no, that was not how it played out. Melodrama is not in their blood. His stoical, rational father never had a taste for ostentation, for the grand gesture. And a reading of the will is not conventional. His sister has long known, in any case, in the finest detail, what his father's last wishes (commands) entailed. Daniel could probably also have found out for himself; he'd simply never been interested in perusing the will.

An email from the lawyer—his father's legal representative, and since their father's death also his sister's—shows up on Daniel's computer. It has numbered paragraphs and a self-consciously formal tone. There is a hitch. Not quite melodrama, not quite a bitter final gesture. And yet. The text of the will is attached to the email, but the lawyer summarises for the sake of convenience. The estate must be liquidated and divided in half. Daniel inherits half and the other half goes to his sister. As far as Daniel's inheritance is concerned, however, there is a condition. He has to visit his cousin Theon in the Free State. Theon, the will explicates, is seriously ill. And he, Daniel, must assist Theon, must do his best to support and encourage his cousin. Daniel is to spend at least a month with him.

Daniel looks out from his desk over the city's heat-hazy, bleached-out greys. Theon is the son of his mother's brother. They last saw each other as children. Daniel cannot recall his father mentioning this cousin in the course of three decades.

Daniel reads the rest of the email. The lawyer assumes that Daniel knows the individual, being a family member. An undertaking to honour the condition is also attached. Daniel is to sign and return it. If he does so, and spends the prescribed period with his cousin, he will be entitled to inherit.

Daniel phones the lawyer. "This condition. Must I really fulfil it?"

"If you want to inherit, I'm afraid, yes. It's somewhat vague, and certain aspects are admittedly difficult to enforce. The only objective criterion is that you must spend at least a month with your cousin. In any case, the estate is complex and will take a year or so to administer." He proposes that Daniel sign the undertaking and pay the visit as soon as possible. What Daniel does while he's with his relative can hardly be monitored, but he should keep to the word and spirit of the stipulation. The lawyer requests that Daniel send him proof of the journey—photos and a sworn affidavit from his cousin, for instance. In the meantime, he will proceed with the administration of the estate as if the condition has been complied with.

Reluctantly, Daniel phones his sister. Over the years, she may have had more dealings with their parents' families than he. Her voice is less self-assured than usual. Perhaps she's more affected by their father's death than Daniel had imagined. Perhaps she is not as perfectly immunised against grief, as untouchable as her seamless existence would suggest.

She doesn't know much. Their cousin had cancer, she remembers, but that was a few years ago, when their father was still compos mentis and probably revised his will for the last time. Of their cousin's misfortune she had heard only incidentally from their father. She herself has not had contact with the family in recent years.

"Why didn't you tell me about this before?" he demands. "About this condition, our father's scheme to bind me from beyond the grave. Why do I have to be told by the lawyer?"

Her voice is pinched. "It was none of my business. It was between you and your father. I was focused on what affects me and my family. Nobody prevented you from finding out for yourself what was in the will." If his father had had a perverse sense of humour, Daniel could perhaps have understood the twist to the bequest, even respected it. But contriving a last trick was not in his father's nature. The old man had never been interested in his in-laws, had apparently never got on with them. When Daniel was still living with his parents, they hardly ever had contact with his mother's now deceased brother. That side of the family were the Free State phantom relations. Farmers, nobodies. Whence this sudden piety?

Daniel remembers a single visit to the Free State farm, when he'd just started high school. It was winter, he recalls, and he and his parents were there for only a few days. His sister was on a hockey tour in the Boland, had managed to avoid the trip. Daniel's aunt had died young; he'd never known her. It was just his uncle and his cousin Theon. All meals were prepared and served by servants. Bedspreads were musty, curtains did not match carpets. He remembers his father's preoccupation during the visit: continually making work phone calls on the farm line, otherwise reading in his bedroom, saying hardly a word at the table in the evenings as leg of lamb or bobotie was served. Daniel followed his father's example, attempting to find ways to show that he didn't belong there either.

Daniel and Theon went for a walk one day. By a spruit lined with poplars, Theon wanted to show him how to play kleilat. Daniel just shook his head. Who on earth still messed about with mud, like children in old-fashioned farm stories on his parents' bookshelves? He sat down on a rock, leaving Theon to break off a switch and burrow in the mud. Daniel now remembers that he'd told Theon to take off his shirt so that he—so he explained—could better observe the technique with the switch. He watched his cousin getting bespattered with mud. His body was shorter, more solid, more tanned than Daniel's. They were in standard six and Theon already had dense down on his upper lip and sun-blond hairs on his arms, all flattened in one direction like grass in the wind. We are better than these people, Daniel thought. They should be grateful to us for visiting them. He walked close to Theon on their way home, trying to feel his heat. At the house Daniel went to lie down in his bedroom to read.

Later in the afternoon, Theon came to fetch him. The sun was setting. Theon lent Daniel a jacket. It was an old military jacket Theon had got from his father. It smelt of man. Daniel wasn't sure that he wanted to put it on. It was cold, so he did. They walked in silence. Around them there was only long grass and, when they passed telephone poles, the crackling of words speeding along the wires. It was the coldest evening Daniel had ever experienced. The jacket scratched his neck and weighed down his shoulders. Theon took him to see the guineafowl sleeping in the poplars. Daniel didn't really know what he was supposed to look at, why he needed to see the dark blotches in the forked branches. Theon bent down to pick up a speckled feather, held it out to Daniel. When Daniel reached for it, Theon pulled it away, then stroked it across the back of Daniel's hand before relinquishing it.

When they left to go back to Cape Town, his cousin stood partly behind his father the farmer, his hair unkempt, his hand lifted in a clumsy wave. Daniel half-smiled from inside the car. He closed his window electronically and waited for the susurration of the dual carriageway beyond the dirt road.

That his mother had also grown up on that farm was never mentioned. She was so perfectly at home among her carefully selected artworks and soft furnishings in Constantia, in the glow of the last afternoon rays over the mountain, that one could not picture her anywhere else. Certainly not as a barefoot girl among tall grass. Still, his mother, Daniel now reflects, harboured divided loyalties. She often phoned her brother from Cape Town, short conversations over the presumably crackly farm line, hand over her other ear. A few times she'd ask Daniel, "Why don't you talk to Theon? Uncle Freek is going to fetch him," and hold out the phone. He'd shake his head and walk away, even though he was thinking of those sunlit hairs on Theon's arm.

Daniel's mother must also have kept him informed about certain family affairs. He knows, for instance, that Theon went to study agriculture in Bloemfontein. Daniel studied political science and languages in Cape Town. Their adult lives had no points of contact. During Daniel's years in London, when he failed to keep in touch even with old friends in South Africa, he forgot about Theon. In any event, since he started commuting between Cape Town and London, his feet have barely been touching ground in either city.

***

Daniel delays the trip for as long as possible. From time to time his annoyance gets the better of him. At one point he resolves to disclaim the inheritance, to defy his father's last gesture with contempt. But after a few months he relents.

Just getting hold of a telephone number for his cousin proves a major undertaking. At length, Daniel tracks down the number of the nearest farmer's cooperative—Daniel had to think hard before he could remember the name of the town. The young woman that Daniel talks to at the co-op is only working there over the holidays and doesn't know

Theon, but she asks her mother, who works there permanently, and she has a number, a landline.

"Are you family?" the mother asks. Daniel shifts the phone to his other ear. He imagines her upper arms emerging sturdy and freckled from her sleeveless dress.

"I am. He's my cousin."

"Oh." Daniel weighs up the charge behind the "Oh".

"How is his health?"

"No idea. I don't really know him." She hesitates. "It's his business, whatever goes on on that farm."

He tries to sound her out subtly, but she says no more. He asks for the name of the farm—Eenzaamheid, loneliness. She also looks up Theon's number in her client files and gives Daniel directions. He now recalls faintly, while she is explaining, how you reach the farm from the town.

Putting down the phone, he decides to simply turn up at his cousin's house—rather that than conducting an awkward long-distance conversation. He will rent a car, take a long road trip. Perhaps the changing landscape will start to soften his heart.

The stretch of dirt road still looks the same, two dusty tracks through blond grass, telephone poles punctuating the route to the farmhouse. He's surprised at how clearly it all comes back to him. The house itself has changed very little, on a superficial assessment: It's still the same low-slung building—from the thirties or forties, he'd guess, then probably extended in the seventies, before his childhood visit. The same steel-framed windows and, it would seem, a new corrugated-iron roof glinting in the winter sun.

Daniel pulls up in the yard in a cloud of dust, the car shrouded in grey. Where he remembers a lawn and flower garden, there is now, he sees on getting out, only hard soil.

On the stoep a woman is seated. One of the labourers, he speculates. Next to her a child is playing with something on the ground. He looked up briefly as Daniel drove up. Now he concentrates on his game again. An older man, probably also a farm labourer, presumably retired, emerges from the front door.

Daniel walks up to them. The dust cloud accompanies him, hovering and then dispersing. A wintry Free State sun hangs low over the tin roof. He nods at the man and woman and bends down to rest his hand on the child's head for a moment. The woman nods, the man nods.

"Theon?" Daniel asks. The woman indicates the inside of the house with her head.

Daniel wipes his feet on the threshold, even though there's no doormat. When his eyes have adapted to the gloom inside, he can see it's the sitting room where he once visited. He even remembers the brown velvet sofas. But apart from that everything looks different. There are mattresses on the floor, and blankets. Pillows. In the furthest corner a boy, probably about ten years old, is lying on a mattress. In the kitchen, he can see through a doorway, a large saucepan is steaming on the stove.

In the door to the passage a figure appears and stops dead. Daniel doesn't recognise him, but it must be his cousin.

"Theon?"

The man frowns, nods. He shakes his head impatiently. "And you are . . . ?"

"I'm your cousin Daniel."

Theon remains standing in the doorway for a few seconds, then turns and disappears into the passage.

Daniel and Theon sit down to supper. At the other end of the table, the man and woman from the stoep sit eating. More people are on the mattresses and sofas. There are, it would seem, five adults and three children living here in the house with Theon.

Daniel sits next to Theon, who has taken the seat at the head of the table. A confusing household, Daniel thinks. It's not clear whose job it is to cook, but a number of saucepans have been simmering on the stove. There is porridge, mutton, cauliflower and pumpkin. There is also a tray with bruised peaches on the table. Everybody serves themselves at will. Daniel's presence apparently doesn't bother anybody. They take no notice of him. One of the women places plates in front of him and his cousin and dishes up pap with slushy meat and vegetables. Only a few lights are burning in the house. The rooms are in semi-darkness. Daniel looks at the mattress in the furthest corner, where the child is still sleeping. He's the only one not eating.

Earlier that afternoon, Daniel had followed Theon through the passage to his bedroom, where Theon sat down silently in a ball-and-claw chair. Stopping in the doorway, Daniel started to explain why he was here. He was candid about the testamentary condition.

"I'm sorry I haven't contacted you in all these years, Theon. But then, you didn't contact me either." Daniel paused for a moment, waiting for a reaction that didn't come. "Sometimes the lives of family members just don't have very much in common. There's no use trying to force connections. To keep contact only because of shared blood."

Theon listened in silence, smiling wryly without facing Daniel directly.

"Well, now it makes sense, you turning up here," he said. "Your inheritance is at stake. Nothing more. We've always been the reject relatives, haven't we? The unmentionables, you could say."

Daniel shrugged. "I don't know about that. Yes, my father was an unbending tyrant. Conceited and prejudice-prone. I had no particular view of you and your family. I was just a child. You and I simply moved in two different spheres. At least I'm honest about my present motives. I suppose I could have turned up here with some story. Pretended I was looking you up to re-establish connections, or to be of assistance—"

"Assistance?"

"I believe you are . . . unwell."

Theon smiled, this time without undue cynicism. "You're about three years late, cousin. I *was* sick, yes. Bone cancer. But I went to hospital a few times, in Bloemfontein, for treatment. Chemotherapy. I've been cured for some time. In remission, at any rate. That was another life, another time." He turned aside to regard the setting sun through the steel-framed window. The wind started up outside, riffling the long grass behind the house. Daniel could feel the cold in the bones of his feet.

"I'm sorry. But I hope you don't hold it against me that I didn't help you, as a family member. I didn't even know there was anything wrong with you." Daniel lifted his shoulders. "To be honest, I would probably not have done anything even if I'd known. We last saw each other as children. And even then, I think, only once." Daniel half-smiled. "It is also the case that as an adult I've tended to somewhat blindly pursue my own interests."

Theon dismissed Daniel's words with a wave of his hand. "I never expected anything from you. Don't expect anything now either. But I *am* irritated with your turning up out of the blue. The Cape Town kin, lowering himself to pay the plaasjapie a visit. Your parents could never bring themselves to have much to do with us, after all." He changed position in his chair, zipping up his jacket. "But I appreciate your honesty."

"As I say, I hardly think you can hold me responsible for my parents' attitude. Especially not my father's. If it makes any difference—I hardly got on with him. I don't share his values and attitudes. It didn't take me long after adolescence to see through him, to understand what he was."

For a moment Daniel also gazed out of the window, at the light diffusing, fading. Theon leant over to switch on a table lamp. It was bright enough to make them both narrow their eyes, looking into each other's faces as if for the first time. Daniel examined the man facing him closely. Nothing had come, he thought, of the promise shown by his cousin's thirteen-year-old body. He was now shapeless, with rounded shoulders and meaty calves. His face was sunburnt, coarse. His biceps, though, were powerful. Noticing his cousin examining him in turn, Daniel wondered what Theon made of his slender body, his skin smooth after years in the northern hemisphere, away from the sun. Daniel looks younger than his years. His cousin looked older than his. They could be from different generations.

"How did it happen," Daniel enquired cautiously, "that you're living in this set-up, with these people?" Daniel gestured vaguely behind him, at the other rooms.

Theon stared at the lamp for a while before starting his story. He and his wife lived on this farm for years with his father. They led a reasonable life. A bit dull, perhaps, and they were hardly affluent, but financially they more or less kept afloat . . .

The woman Daniel had met earlier on the stoep came into the room. "This is Malefu," Theon said. "And this is Daniel," he told her. These two sentences were in Afrikaans, for Daniel's benefit. Then the two of them exchanged a few further sentences in Sotho.

"Food is ready," she said in Afrikaans. She seemed irritated, looking at Daniel as if he was here to deprive her of something, before disappearing again.

Daniel followed Theon to the kitchen. And now they're sitting here, at the old family table, with all the labourers. Or family, friends, housemates, whatever they are. They mutter in an undertone in Sotho. Turning to Daniel, Theon continues his story. He and his wife couldn't have children. In retrospect, perhaps not such a bad thing. They stayed here with his father, guests of the master of the house. Later, much later, when his father's health deteriorated, he stayed with them, was *their* guest, needing their care. Malefu moved in to help. And then Theon himself fell ill. Cancer of the hip. He started travelling to Bloemfontein for chemotherapy sessions. It was a bad year. Their harvests failed. And it wasn't clear that Theon would survive; the prognosis was not good . . .

The front door opens. A young man enters from outside with a load of firewood in his arms. Daniel doesn't know who he is. Theon hasn't introduced him to anyone except Malefu. The man starts arranging logs in the fireplace.

After the third chemotherapy session, Theon continues, when he was lying here in the house vomiting constantly, all the windows closed against the winter dust, his wife announced that she was leaving him. She had for a long time, she confessed, been having a relationship with the town butcher. And now the two of them were moving to another town. Just the thought of meat saws and the smell of blood made Theon vomit immediately, he says, before his wife could complete her sentence. She refused to look at Theon. "It's too much, all of this," she said. "It's just too much."

"Ah yes, the hardy boervrou," he said, through the strings of saliva, "standing by her man, through thick and thin."

She arranged for yet another labourer to move into the house to see to his needs. The care of his father would continue as before. She'd bring medication for Theon on a weekly basis. She was only two hours away. She hoped, she said, that God—and perhaps one day Theon as well—would forgive her, but in this house she couldn't remain for another second. Barely a day later, she left for a place where nobody knew her and the butcher, and they could leave the scandal behind.

His father died a week later. Two of the labourers' sons carried Theon in a chair to the family graveyard. They were the only ones at the burial. And a pastor from the township. Theon's wife never once returned to check on his condition, or to bring his medicine as she'd promised. She simply abandoned him and his half-dead father here among desiccated mealies and the billowing grass.

The fire is lit. The wood crackles and the room starts to fill with smoke, as if the flue is blocked. Then it flares up properly and the chimney starts extracting the smoke. Daniel picks up his spoon; the food is already lukewarm. Theon's spoon is still resting next to his plate.

Shortly thereafter, Theon continues, he let all the labourers move in. Why not? There was only one family left on the farm. In the preceding years he hadn't been able to afford many labourers. And their housing was substandard, with thin walls and unpainted tin roofs. Icy in winter and sweltering in summer. "They looked after me." Taking up his spoon, Theon starts eating abstractedly. "They were the ones who helped me survive when my wife decided she'd had enough and moved out. After my death everything will go to them. In the meantime I live here quite happily. I have a family of sorts. I am surrounded by children. I am healthy. Contented, even."

Abruptly, he glances at the other end of the room. Then, getting up, he goes to crouch by the mattress where the boy has been lying all day. Theon says something which Daniel can't hear, apparently in Sotho; the child turns his head to him. Next to the mattress is a plate that one of the women put down there a while ago. Theon takes a spoonful of food, offers it to the boy. He turns away his head. Theon talks to him again gently, placing a hand on his shoulder. He stands up, comes back to the table.

Theon looks at Daniel's half-eaten plate of food. "It's simply too much," Daniel says. He pushes away the plate. "More than I'm used to." A young woman comes to take the plate to the scullery.

"Quite contented, like I say," Theon says, reflectively. "I don't give a damn about the rest." He gestures at everything around him. "The farm, the tractor rusting away. The corner posts collapsing, the exhausted soil. What I am sorry about is that I neglected my cattle. Some were stolen, a few had too little grazing and died. The rest I sent to auction. Too late—I didn't get much for them.

"Let's go out," he says abruptly. He gets up, takes a key from the sideboard, says something to one of the women. Daniel takes note of Theon's tone. Maybe he calls the people living with him his family, but they're evidently something between servants and family. Theon only really talks to them to issue orders. And he still hasn't introduced Daniel to anybody other than Malefu. The rest hover about anonymously, like ghosts.

Daniel follows Theon out. As he closes the front door, his eyes meet those of the little boy lying in the corner. What is wrong with the child? He hasn't got up once since Daniel's arrival.

They get into Theon's bakkie. On their way to town in the cold cab, neither says anything. Theon stops in front of the largest structure in the village, a hotel. When they get out of the bakkie, Daniel stops dead. He looks at the name over the entrance—steel lettering, a thirties font. Daniel smiles, shaking his head. An enduring mystery cleared up in an instant.

Five years before his father's death, his mother fell ill and died within months. He came from London, staying in his city flat and driving to Constantia once a day to see her, at times when he was sure not to find his sister visiting from Paarl. In his mother's last days, when she was heavily sedated with morphine, he sat down next to her bed. His sister was there then, and his father. He'd wished he could keep vigil on his own, be granted an opportunity to accompany her on the path of light, in silence, up to the point where it became too blinding and he had to turn back.

His father had retreated into his study, hardly emerging. An atmosphere of high tension seeped through his door, filling the house. His absence was even worse than his presence. But most of all, his sister's clamorous, weeping excess sullied Daniel's last hours with his mother. Her mourning, he was convinced, was all on the surface, a thing of smudged makeup and the extra-soft tissues she kept crumpling between her fingers.

Mercifully, at the moment of passing Daniel was alone with his mother. His exhausted sister had lain down in the adjacent room for a few minutes; his father was still in his study. And Daniel called nobody. His mother had, without opening her eyes, turned her head by a few degrees, trying to say something. Daniel lowered his ear close to her face.

"Now, all of you, go and have a nice meal at the Imperial Hotel."

Her breath failed. Then, unexpectedly, she took two shallow breaths. Then, after a while, one more. Then nothing.

Ever since then, Daniel has frequently wondered about the Imperial. He was not aware of any such hotel. Was there in fact such a place? Was it merely an abstraction, embodying her aspirational impulses of accumulation and display? Her hankering after elegance? Or was the hotel incidental, and her utterance just a last—desperate, inevitably doomed—attempt to snare him and his sister and father into something resembling a family unit?

Whatever the truth, in the intervening years he'd searched for an Imperial Hotel in every city he visited; if there was one, which almost without exception there was, he checked into it. Sometimes it was the best—and priciest—hotel in town. Sometimes he had to compromise considerably in terms of quality. In New York, in particular, the ritual was a bit of an ordeal. He stayed for one night in a highly dubious Imperial Hotel, in an unillustrious part of Brooklyn. The old bloodstains on the towels, and the sound in the early hours, somewhere, of fists striking a human body—or so it seemed—were eventually too much. *That* his mother would not have wished upon him. After one sleepless night there he moved to Manhattan, where the Regency Hotel was, he thought, near enough in spirit to his project.

Was it a wry kind of tribute to his dying mother, who hadn't been able to take any of her carefully selected and impeccably curated treasures with her, these sojourns in the Imperial Hotels of the world, always on his own, regardless of quality or price? Was it an ironic gesture? He couldn't tell what it signified. Its import, he thought, would perhaps crystallise incrementally in his mind.

But here he is, looking up at the façade of a building in a Free State town. And the letters over the front door unambiguously spell it out: *Imperial Hotel. The* Imperial Hotel. His mother, he now knows, had not in her last moments cherished dreams of grandiosity or luxury. No, she'd returned to the world of her youth, to the simpler life she'd known as a child. Her final vision was something like a Sunday lunch after church in the local hotel—a family sitting down to an old-fashioned starched tablecloth, the savour of leg of lamb and gravy and, beneath that, the scent of long switches of dry grass inexpungibly permeating their clothes.

Turning back on the steps, Theon frowns at Daniel, standing there. "What are you gaping at?" Daniel just shakes his head, enters the hotel with Theon.

They are greeted by a white plastic kitten with a waving paw on the unstaffed reception desk. "Fathom that," Daniel says, pointing at the cat. "A Japanese lucky charm, in a plattelandse Free State hotel."

"If you stay here long enough, you'll find plenty of things to surprise you."

After ordering beer from the bar, they sit down at a table. Theon greets a few people in passing. A few men come over to greet him. Others, Daniel notes, turn their backs on seeing him.

Daniel gestures at the room. "Are these your friends?"

Theon shrugs. "You could say so, I suppose. Some of them, at least. A lot of them disapprove of the fact that I allow my people—everyone who worked for us over the years—to live in the house like that. They think I'm a disgrace. I can't do anything about that. There are still quite a few of the old types around here. They'll never change."

For a while they drink their beers in silence. Against one wall, a flatscreen television is screening a provincial rugby match.

"If your father was such a tyrant, Daniel, why such a condition in his will? Why would he want to help me?"

Daniel takes a sip of beer. "I don't have the answer to that. Perhaps a show of piety to my mother. But I have my doubts. It was hardly the most loving of marriages. My question is:

Why couldn't he have helped you in a more direct way? He could have left you money, for instance. Why involve me? Did you ever hear from him when you were ill?"

Theon shakes his head. He looks back at the reception desk, smiling at the waving kitten. He lifts a hand, returns the wave. The gesture is childlike, like that of a boy. Out of keeping with his heavy frame. "You know," he says, "I've always wanted to go to Japan. Lots of places, actually, but Japan in particular."

"Well, it's never too late." Daniel takes another sip of beer. "I haven't been to Japan myself. But don't think you can escape yourself by going wandering. Distances have shrunk so much nowadays. The world is too small to get away. Wherever you go, your own blood keeps flowing in your veins. In the most remote corner of the earth, your own heart still beats in your breast."

They order another beer. For the most part they drink in silence, feigning interest in the rugby match. By now we must have exhausted every single subject we could conceivably have in common, Daniel thinks. And he's supposed to spend a whole month here. The men at the bar keep getting rowdier. In the foyer the cat waves on ceaselessly, with perfect rhythm.

In the bakkie on the way home, they listen to the tarmac under the wheels.

Theon looks at Daniel. "You know, your visit is a bit of a godsend."

"How come? You're healthy now, aren't you? You have your farm, and your new family. You don't need me."

"I'm healthy, yes. But there is Motlalepule. Motlale, we call him . . ."

Daniel looks at his cousin quizzically. They're both breathing vapour in the cabin. Theon turns on cold air to evaporate the condensation on the windscreen.

"The boy. Malefu's child." Theon changes gears, slowing down to avoid a pothole. "The one who lies on a mattress all day."

"I have wondered about him, yes. What's the matter with him?"

"He's the one who's unwell now. A very rare form of blood cancer. Aggressive, untreatable. I've had him in a private hospital in Bloemfontein. Many times. Did all the tests, tried every treatment they could offer. Without success." He grimaces. "Of course, Malefu thinks I made him ill. That I infected him. She won't listen to my explanations."

Theon changes to a higher gear, accelerating. "In the last few years, since everybody moved in with me, I've been raising that boy as if he were my own."

Daniel waits for more.

"Like my own son," Theon says.

When Theon falls silent, Daniel asks: "And how could I be of use?"

"He needs different treatment. In the right hospital."

"Surely Bloemfontein's hospitals are as good as any?"

"In this country, yes. There's a new form of treatment, the oncologist said. Experimental stuff. But it's not in South Africa yet. Early indications are that it's a kind of wonder cure."

"So where, then?"

Theon changes up another gear. "It's been developed in Japan, this new medicine. And the doctor in charge of the clinical trials is in Tokyo."

"So, can one import the medicine? These trials are often international."

"No, it's only available in Japan. They combine chemotherapy with traditional stuff. An extract, among other things, of a flower that only grows there."

"And it's your idea that I fund it all?"

"Well, you're about to inherit a pile of money."

"You forget that the estate hasn't been sorted out yet. It's going to take months. Or longer. And then there's this awkward condition . . ."

"The condition you can meet. You can stay here for a month. And while it's all being sorted out, you've got enough money, I'm sure. The inheritance will refill your coffers. So, that's my suggestion: If you provide money for the trip, and the treatment, then I'll help you to get your money from your father's estate. Deal?"

Daniel looks at the pale grass in the headlights. It seems to be vibrating frenetically, tens of thousands of blades flitting past. A trip to Tokyo was maybe not a bad idea. Then he wouldn't have to spend so much time here in the emptiness of the Free State. And he's sure he could write something on Japan for a British broadsheet. A Sunday supplement. Something obliquely related to Tokyo architecture, maybe, off the top of his head. He's read a lot about it before. Something, perhaps, about lives in the city's architectural crevices, the in-between spaces. He'll start with *The Observer*. He'll get in touch with his contact there soon, tomorrow even.

Theon slows down; they turn onto the two-track road leading to the farmhouse.

"Okay," Daniel says. "Deal."

Daniel has been allocated the bedroom next to Theon's. He lies awake, listening to the sleeping sounds of strangers in various parts of the house. He gets up noiselessly, walks in his socks down the cold passageway. In the sitting room he passes behind the sofa, careful not to step on a sleeper or make a sound. He switches on the screen of his phone, shines the feeble light on the little body. The child is lying on his tummy. His breathing is shallow. His shirt has rucked up in the cold. Then Daniel catches the mother's eye. Malefu, on the adjacent mattress. She is awake, staring expressionlessly up at him. Then she puts out a hand to pull the blanket over the child, covering half his head. As if to protect him from Daniel's gaze. Or from the light shining from the palm of his hand.

* * *

The breath of the sleeping passengers hover cloud-like in the aircraft cabin. Daniel feels short of oxygen. In his mind's eye, he sees a ghost aircraft: a fuselage—without a single living creature on board, just a pile of suffocated bodies—flying on and on until the fuel runs out. He imagines urgent, abrupt voices crackling over the radio from flight-control towers, imagines the sound echoing through the cabin, washing over all the dead bodies. When he closes his eyes, he sees the flying grave plummeting down towards the lights of a sprawling Asian city . . .

Motlale is one of the passengers sleeping. The boy is lying diagonally across Theon's lap. Theon and Daniel are awake. They're an hour from Hong Kong, where they connect to Tokyo. It took more than a month to get the child a passport, to obtain the required medical reports from Bloemfontein, to make arrangements with the National Cancer Centre in Tokyo and to get visas. Motlale will be admitted to the cancer centre for a period of nearly three weeks. If the treatment has the desired effect, they will have to return to Tokyo after two months, and, if there are further improvements, again after a further two months.

While the arrangements were taking shape, Daniel fell in with the rhythms of life on Eenzaamheid. Or adjusted himself to the lack of rhythm. Theon slept in one bedroom,

Daniel in another. The third bedroom had been converted into Theon's study. The rest of the people all slept in the sitting room and kitchen, close to the stove and fireplace. In the early mornings there were voices and movement, then the smell of pap from the kitchen, the sun slanting in through the windows and slowly warming the house, and when you went outside, the brilliance that made you reach for sunglasses: frost and patches of ice, white grass, a brittle-blue sky with fleecy clouds, the silver roof of the house.

Before breakfast Daniel usually went for a walk to the spruit lined with poplars, where Theon had once wielded a kleilat. Now Daniel was rigid with cold, a cap pulled down low over his ears. Back at the house, he'd have coffee and pap in the sun on the stoep with the rest of the inhabitants. He had unpacked his suitcase on the first morning, arranging the books he'd brought with him on the bedside table. During the day he sat reading for hours in the sun, in his room or on the stoep. In the warmer hours of the day, once the frost had melted, he'd take another solitary walk, sitting down on a rocky outcrop or just in the grass with his book. A kind of tranquillity came over him, such as he had not experienced in many years.

In the evenings he and his cousin would sit in silence or watch television with the rest of the household. Soccer mainly, or game shows. Traditional music programmes. Or American rap. At night there was always a fire in the fireplace. Daniel drove into town every few days to buy food. On the farm there were egg-laying hens and a vegetable garden. But milk and flour he had to buy; meat from the butcher. Daniel took a close look at the present butcher, as if he might be the one who'd absconded with his cousin's wife. At the house, Malefu or one of the younger women did the cooking: stews and porridge and vegetables.

On the day that Motlale was due to leave for Japan with Daniel and Theon, Malefu had pressed her lips together and locked herself in the bathroom. She refused to say goodbye to them or to her son. Daniel did not intervene.

Because the boy seemed so limp and feeble when they boarded the plane in Johannesburg, some of the cabin staff came to enquire about his state of health.

"He's fine," Daniel said. "He's just tired." They had to be careful. There were special procedures to be followed before seriously ill passengers were allowed to fly. They hadn't had the stomach for all that red tape. And what a disaster it would have been, had the airline refused Motlale the right to fly.

Motlale speaks only Sotho; Daniel can't communicate with him. Not that the boy is in any state to make small talk. Theon is fluent in the language, exchanging reassuring sentences with Motlale from time to time, explaining things, answering questions. The boy is curious about all the novel experiences. Except for the hospital visits in Bloemfontein, he's never been away from the farm, Theon explains. But the urge to look around and absorb impressions is thwarted by his weakness. In the week before their departure, he visibly lost weight and moved with increasing difficulty.

Theon thumbs the pages of a travel guide and other books on Japan that he's brought along. He's particularly fascinated by the information on Japanese seasons. "Did you know that Japanese seasons are divided up far more precisely than ours? They have twenty-four of them, and each one is divided into three again. Seventy-two in all."

Daniel is actually trying to sleep, though he knows he won't succeed. He read for a while at first, then watched half a movie, an infantile romantic comedy. Now he's squirming in his chair with a stiff neck. He has no choice but to listen to his cousin.

"So what season—micro-season—will it be when we get there?"

"Well, every little season is about five days long. We're arriving during Shōsho, the three short seasons of moderate heat. While we're there, the warm winds will blow, the first lotuses will flower, and the eagles will learn to fly. Then comes Taisho, the season of stronger heat. The empress trees spread their seeds—"

The captain interrupts Theon, announces heavy turbulence ahead. Seatbelts click into place. Not long afterwards the shaking starts. Motlale wakes up, clinging to Theon. He presses a hand to the boy's chest, says something.

"What are you telling him?"

"I'm telling him that the shaking is just inside his chest, that his heart is rejoicing because we're going to a place where he will get well."

Daniel isn't sure that Theon should be fostering such hopes in the child.

Tokyo is hot and humid. Theon has dark patches under his arms when they deposit their suitcases in the hotel lobby. The hotel—the Imperial, naturally; Daniel did the booking—is in Ginza, which seems pretty soulless to Daniel, indistinguishable from the commercial centres of other cities he knows. The hotel, too, is like any expensive international hotel, luxurious and lacking individual charm.

Their room is spacious, with two double beds. Motlale will sleep next to Theon in his bed. The boy is exhausted. He goes to stand by the window, gazing out. He clearly doesn't know what to make of this new world. On the way here, he rested his forehead on the window of the taxi and gaped at the cityscape. What a bleak, barren, funereal city, Daniel thought.

When the boy has gone to bed, Daniel also goes to stand at their bedroom window, looking out over the imperial palace complex. In what strange circumstances is he embroiled? He resents his father, and the period during which his dwindling intellect prevented him from updating his will. But, if it hadn't been that, his father would have found some other way to punish Daniel, would have thought up some other last directive.

Daniel sighs, turns back to the room. Motlale is curled up on the bed. Daniel feels a mixture of impatience and compassion for the child. From tomorrow he will be in hospital for the full duration of their stay, for treatment and monitoring. To Daniel's relief, he has to admit.

Theon and Motlale are both sleeping as if dead. Daniel stretches out diagonally on his own bed, allowing the breeze of the air conditioner to revive him. At last he drifts into restless sleep, the city's unfamiliar rhythms disrupting his slumber.

Daniel and Theon queue in an alleyway, waiting to be admitted to a popular little ramen restaurant. The alley is so narrow that Theon has to turn sideways to accommodate his shoulders. Above them hang tangles of power cords. Against the walls there are wires and pipes and air-conditioning units. It's like being trapped in the entrails of an animal.

In front of them in the queue, at the end of the alley, is a man with a blind friend. Every now and then the blind man puts one foot into the street in front of him, as if feeling his way. He must obviously be able to hear the traffic rushing past, scooters whizzing by at close quarters, but it's as if he is perversely defying them, or has a death wish. Time and again his friend has to pull him back into the alley.

Theon regards the man's blind compulsion with increasing

alarm. "That's enough," he says suddenly, his face panicked. "We have to get out of this trench *now*."

"A moment's patience," Daniel says. And at last they're beckoned up a narrow staircase. They pay for their food at a vending machine and take a seat at the counter. The dishes that are served are flavoursome and steaming, covered with a film of seaweed.

They are hungry, initially exchanging few words while eating. The noodles are satisfyingly rubbery and substantial. Earlier that day they took Motlale to the cancer centre. They saw the oncologist, one Doctor Yoshikawa. His English was reasonable, but his voice so soft that at times he was barely audible. The boy sat wide-eyed, gazing at the Japanese hospital staff. They had wondered, said the doctor, how they would communicate with him. He can read and write a bit of English, Theon explained. They would write things on a whiteboard for Motlale, it was agreed. For the rest they would make do with gestures. Theon need not be concerned, Yoshikawa said. They would look after him well. There was a television in Motlale's room, and they had a huge library of cartoons for him to choose from. And they'd give him Western food. He would be assessed, and treatment would commence the following day.

Before they left, Theon spoke to Motlale in Sotho, comforting him, promising that they'd return the following day—or so Theon translated for Daniel as they walked away. Daniel glanced back. Motlale was watching their departure anxiously, sitting stock-still.

That is what Daniel is thinking about as he slurps up the noodles. Theon's thoughts are elsewhere. After the first few mouthfuls, the edge apparently taken off his hunger, he turns to Daniel. "Do you have any idea how much you hurt me?"

Daniel lowers his chopsticks. He feels disoriented. The

time difference between Japan and South Africa is taking its toll. "What are you talking about?"

"Those moments of closeness. When we were children." Daniel shakes his head. Ramen soup gleams on Theon's chin. "You sitting there watching me digging clay in the spruit. I'd never played kleilat before. It wasn't the kind of thing I did. It was a show for you. I just wanted to show you *something* . . . I thought: That's the kind of thing you'd expect plaasjapies to do. And then, later, when we went to look for guineafowl. I really just wanted to walk with you, have you to myself. For what and why I don't know exactly."

Daniel wipes the soup from his chin. This is all out of the blue. He looks at Theon, surprised at his cousin's unguarded confrontation with his childhood instincts. How did Theon come to talk so readily about it? Perhaps grave illness—facing death head-on—does that to you; your patience with chit-chat dries up. Or perhaps it's just this foreign space that's making Theon feel untethered and liberated.

For a while they carry on eating noodles wordlessly. Theon, Daniel reflects, is retrospectively imbuing his childhood impressions with meaning in the light of later insights.

"We were simple-minded children, Theon." Daniel speaks with his mouth full. "The products—victims—of our parents, our worlds."

"And yet. I felt this urgent need to engage with you, even though I was a child. After that single visit of yours, I told my father so many times, every time he spoke to your mother on the phone, I also want to talk. With you. But we never exchanged another word."

Theon is eating faster and faster. Daniel wonders if it's jet lag that's making his cousin so emotional, escalating his mood like this.

Theon continues. "Do you think it was fun for me to spend

my days there in the veld? Later, to farm? Plant mealies, feed cattle? To drive to the co-op in my bakkie, collect mail from the village? All of it under my father's thumb?"

The next four diners are already being beckoned up the stairs. There's pressure to eat up. This is a place where you wolf down your meal efficiently and yield your place to other hungry people. Hardly a space that promotes profound conversation.

"Surely those things are not my fault, Theon. I didn't determine the course of your life." Daniel stops chewing for a moment. "What is it that you want, Theon?" Daniel places his chopsticks across his bowl. "What would fill the gaps? What do you *desire*?"

If Daniel had thought that these questions would stop his cousin in his tracks, he was wrong. Theon is not to be put off his stride. "I don't know. I don't know what I need. All that is clear to me is that everything, all my life, has been founded on the wrong assumptions, you could say. I never found my balance. Was always on the wrong foot, blindsided. Nothing ever felt right. As if I was always wearing a stranger's clothes.

"And my father who lingered for so long, who just kept lying there in the house . . . " His eyes flick sideways, as if something has occurred to him. "Do you know," he interrupts himself, "that up to the age of eighty my father was stronger than me? Until he was confined to his bed. Later, when he'd lost his wits, when he tried to resist when I bathed him, I could for the first time make him do what *I* wanted, make his body bend and move like a rigid doll's. It was such a relief when he lost his marbles, when he couldn't control anything any more."

All the while, Theon is eating with abandon, talking with his mouth full of food. Initially he struggles with the chopsticks, then switches to his porcelain spoon. Daniel feels tiny splashes against his arms when Theon's noodles slip back into his soup. Daniel, for his part, is too taken aback at this confessional deluge, at the swift succession of subjects, to carry on eating.

"I used to get news of you from my father. How you were working as a consultant, and later for newspapers, in England. Living in London I thought: Maybe a life like that would suit me better. But once you get trapped in one spot . . . " Theon shakes his head.

Daniel takes up his chopsticks again, lifts a mouthful of noodles to his lips, then lowers it. "Do you think my existence was—*is*—ideal? That it's a glamorous sort of life, staying in some random world city? Or shuttling between cities and countries? To lead such a meandering, drifting sort of life? Everything starts to seem so distant and abstract, as if you're looking the wrong way through a zoom lens."

Theon says nothing, just slurps up the last of his noodles. When that's done, he shreds the sheet of seaweed, the size of half a foolscap page, into fine strips and eats all of that as well. He drains his glass of water. "I could eat noodles like that every evening."

"Come," Daniel says. He pushes away his half-eaten plate of food. "Let's go and have a drink."

Daniel takes Theon to the gay area. Most of the dozens of tiny bars are so cramped that no more than nine or ten people can fit into them. Daniel and Theon enter one, shrinking themselves, sitting down on two high stools.

They both drink vodka. Too much, too fast. One of the Japanese barmen joins them. He can speak scarcely a word of English, but apparently it's his job to amuse them, or at any rate offer them some distraction, make them feel at home. Like a male geisha. They nod at each other in turn instead of talking. There is more silence than speech; they don't understand each other. When the intimate silence gets too oppressive, and Daniel and Theon take their leave, the man accompanies them outside to see them off. He greets them formally, bowing.

They go into another bar. This one is full of young Japanese men who take note of the two Westerners entering. Taking a seat, Daniel orders two beers. Theon goes to the toilet. Two young men come in, go to wait at the toilet door. One of them is drunk—unsteady on his feet, his movements fluid. He jokes with his friend. When Theon emerges, the young man's eyes open wide. He exclaims something and throws his arms around Theon's neck. He opens his mouth and starts kissing Theon. Theon seems less taken aback, less defensive, than Daniel would have expected. For a moment Theon stands still, letting the young man have his way, even tilting his head as if to accommodate the kiss. The young man's friend pulls him away. Theon is standing there, his mouth slightly agape, like a wound. Surprised, he touches his lower lip. The two Japanese men stumble into the toilet cubicle and close the door.

Theon sits down next to Daniel, dazed.

"You okay?"

Theon nods. He seems bewildered now, doesn't speak. When they've drunk their beer they leave.

Daniel looks at Theon while they're walking. "It's not the end of the world, being kissed by a man, you know. Your masculinity hasn't been irreversibly contaminated."

"You don't understand," says Theon. "I really hoped that was it—what my problem had always been. Hoped it might be the solution."

"What?"

"That I'm gay. But now I know. It did nothing for me, that

kiss. A while ago I started thinking: Maybe I want to sleep with a man. That would explain everything. And now? Now there's no solution."

Daniel looks at his cousin, at this moment the one still point in the turning world. He imagines Theon in one of the love hotels that are so ubiquitous in this part of town. In a room with a forest theme: lush tropical wallpaper, leaves rustling in the air conditioner's breeze, subdued lighting. And, when you switch off the light, there are insect sounds on the speakers. He can see it all, also his bulky cousin in the midst of this luxuriance. What he cannot imagine at all is the person with Theon there in the shadowy bed. That figure remains an empty space.

Motlale is seated on a chair. Amber fluid is seeping into his arm through a plastic tube: his second treatment. Theon has brought him Japanese sweets in rice paper, but he's not eating them. Theon has his booklet with its finely differentiated Japanese seasons on his lap. He is reading aloud to Motlale, interpreting in Sotho as he reads, showing the boy the illustrations. Sometimes Theon gets stuck searching for the Sotho word before carrying on again. Daniel follows Theon's finger sporadically finding its place on the page.

Risshun, Daniel reads over Theon's shoulder. *The beginning of spring: The east wind melts the snow, the warblers start singing in the mountains, fish appear from the ice.*

The doctor comes in, beckons to Theon and Daniel. They accompany him to the corner of the treatment room. They sit down on the edges of three chairs, their heads together.

The doctor speaks in his low voice, rocking slightly. Theon asks if they've noticed any response to the medication yet. "No, it's far too early. A few early side-effects, yes. But we have to carry on. We're going to do everything we can to save him. To lose a child . . . " He looks at Theon. "Is it your child?"

Theon does not say, "No, it's not my child." He waits for the doctor to continue.

"In 2011 I had to give up both of mine," says the doctor. He smiles faintly, nodding.

Theon sits up straight, withdrawing his head from the little triangle. "That is an unbearable loss. How did that happen?"

Doctor Yoshikawa hesitates momentarily. "Up to 2011 I lived in Sendai. I was head of oncology in a hospital there. On the eleventh of March that year there was that major earthquake. I was at the hospital as usual. My wife and the two children were at home. Our house was situated in a low-lying area, near the coast. After the earthquake I couldn't phone; the cellphone towers had been destroyed. I couldn't leave the hospital either. We were busy assessing patients, trying to save the most severely ill and move the others . . . "

Doctor Yoshikawa's eyes are on the transparent sack suspended over Motlale from a stand. He addresses a nurse in Japanese as she walks past in the passage. She comes in, adjusts a valve on Motlale's drip.

The doctor has fallen silent. "You were talking about the earthquake," Theon says. His cousin's pushiness makes Daniel uneasy.

Doctor Yoshikawa continues. "They were swallowed by the water, my family. By the tsunami. Only the next day could I reach the place where my house had been. A large fishing vessel had been stranded in the centre of the town when the waters receded. A good thirty or forty metres long. They were no longer there, my wife and children. Not even their bodies. The sea had come to claim them, in their own home."

Like Theon, the oncologist and Daniel now sit back in their chairs.

"An impossible loss," Theon says. "I don't know what to say. Is that why you came to Tokyo?" Daniel cringes at Theon's forthright questions. The doctor seems to find it difficult to speak.

"I couldn't live in my home again. It was . . . hankai." He looks at the nurse, who is noting something in Motlale's patient file. "How do you say that in English?"

"Condemned," says the nurse, without looking up. "Or, no." She puts down the file, lifting her head. "Half destroyed." She leaves the room.

The doctor nods. "Half destroyed, yes. At the time I thought: I am also hankai. But, and I'm more and more sure of this, the soul is strong. You don't remain a ruin forever."

He nods, smiling faintly. "It was strange," he says. "The people who survived that day, the eleventh of March, were those dying in hospital. The healthy ones drowned in their homes. I could save the ones at death's door; but not my children, whose lives lay before them."

He gets up, double-checks Motlale's pressure valve, smiles and bows slightly to the boy. He closes the door gently behind him as he leaves. His departure is as unexpected as his narrative.

"The eleventh of March," says Theon after a while. He opens his book to a bookmarker, consults a table. "It falls in Keichitsu. The time of the awakening of the insects—when the hibernating bugs emerge, the first peach blossoms appear and the chrysalises turn into butterflies."

Theon, used to Free State beef, is now tucking with gusto into raw fish, all kinds of pickled things, and rice wine. Daniel's own belly rebels. He, who used to be so adventurous with food, who would scour cities for unusual ingredients, who would experiment so devotedly in front of his stove—sometimes cooking for friends, more often for stranger lovers—simply cannot eat any more Japanese food. He feels increasingly hungry, in desperation starts to seek out American hamburger chains.

"All these things tasting vaguely of the sea, of fish and seaweed," he tells Theon, feeling his abdomen. "My body doesn't identify them as edible. My digestive system is suddenly hankering after simplicity, the hinterland. After vegetables from the dark soil and the flesh of animals roaming the dry hills."

Theon laughs. "You're so melodramatic. You, coming from that miserable city with the sea on both sides."

During the day, in between the times spent with Motlale in the hospital, Daniel and his cousin visit nearby tourist spots. They go to the Tsukiji fish market, as well as the Hama-rikyū Gardens, where they kneel shoeless to drink tea in a wooden building jutting out over the water. They wander through temples, stroll in Ginza. One evening they go to Shinjuku, even though it discomfits Theon to be so far from the hospital. As they move through the forest of neon, Theon seems more and more hypnotised by the light. They walk into a pachinko salon—a place with an ocean of gambling machines raising the most incredible racket. Men sit on their own in the din and glare, each engrossed in his own machine, usually with ear plugs. One of them just sits there, doing nothing, the machine flickering and rattling in front of him. His fingers are stuffed into his ears, his eyes tightly shut. He doesn't touch the machine, but doesn't get up and leave either. Daniel stares at him, his hands over his own ears, until it feels as if he's starting to dissolve in the deafening noise. He takes his cousin by the arm, drags him out.

Theon wanders into a shop selling domestic appliances. Everything is white, the light is brighter than anything Daniel has ever experienced. A young woman wearing a little-girl outfit is proclaiming something in an infantile voice through a megaphone while brandishing some pamphlets. Around her neck is a large satin bow, as on a teddy bear or bunny. Her white platform boots are laced up to the knees. On the pamphlets are pictures of ovens and fridges. Theon stands hypnotised, gazing at the rows and rows of super-efficient, blinding machines. Perhaps his mother would feel at home here, it occurs to Daniel from nowhere, here where fulfilment is to be found in the perfect washing machine.

They return to the hotel. Theon sits paging through his travel guides. Daniel lies down on the bed, letting the air conditioner cool his sweaty body. He's made hardly any headway on his proposed essay on the architecture of the city. And it's been some time since he tried his hand at fiction. His father— or his father's death—briefly revived the impulse to write. But soon the reservoirs ran dry. Perhaps it's his cousin's fault. Or the godforsaken fields of grass. Or Japan. Who knows. He constantly feels half paralysed here, as if he can't shake off the jet lag. His thoughts and his emotional echo chambers are occupied by Motlale's treatment and the ebb and flow of his cousin's moods. Tomorrow, he promises himself, he'll initiate his research on the essay, or at least his thinking, even if it means shutting himself off from his cousin and the sick child.

When Daniel wakes from a nap, his cousin is standing by the window, guide in hand, absorbed in the signs of the seasons. Apparently Theon finds it soothing, the metronomic measurement of time and seasonal changes. Perhaps it's because he is so used to the rhythms of the Free State grasslands. So there he stands by the window, reading the vicissitudes of nature aloud to the whole city, to the buildings and the trains and the commuters scurrying about like soundless robots: "Rikka. The beginning of summer in May. The frogs start singing, the worms wriggle from the soil, the bamboo sprouts." Then suddenly it's Kanro, time of the cold dew: "The wild geese return, the chrysanthemums bloom, the crickets chirp outside the door." Theon does not consider the seasons patiently and chronologically. He flips back to early summer, forward to winter. He jumbles them up, as if making them into a poem. What he reads out no longer bears any relation to the country's true calendar, to the finely calibrated seasons of the present. He jumps around, selecting the micro-seasons that sound best to him, curating them.

Daniel and Theon are back in the hospital, in Motlale's room. Today Motlale is not in the mood for the needle and poisons. He resists when the nurses want to move him to the treatment room. When at last they manage to get him into his wheelchair and take him there, he protests vociferously in Sotho when they try to insert the needle in his arm. To the great surprise of Daniel, who has followed with Theon, he utters a few words in Japanese.

"Itai!" Motlale exclaims, and "Sawaranaide!"

"Ouch!" and "Don't touch me," a nurse translates when Daniel asks. Motlale doesn't want to sit in a chair, waiting for the medicine to be dripped into him; he moves about. The radius of his circle is equal to the length of the tube attached at one end to the bag and at the other end to his wrist. He is like a chained dog. He complains, yelling things in Sotho. For the first time since Daniel has met him, the boy cries. He starts tugging at the tube. A nurse has to hold him down so that the needle doesn't get dislodged.

Daniel takes Theon aside. "I suppose we should have anticipated that this trip would upset the child," Daniel says to his cousin. "The strangeness of it all. All the toxins they're pumping into him. Look how terrified he is, how bewildered. I keep wondering: Wouldn't it have been better for him to have stayed there in the farmhouse, among the people he knows, in the place he knows? Is all this really worth the trouble?"

Theon does not reply. He turns round, takes Motlale in his arms, calms him, comforts him. He sits down with the boy on his lap, as close to the window as the tube permits, and starts teaching him the descriptions of the 72 seasons. By now, Theon knows almost all the seasons by heart.

Daniel can hear Motlale insisting on Theon's repeating the phenomena of one micro-season over and over again. He asks Theon about this. "It is Seimei he wants to hear about," says Theon. "The brightest days—when the swallows return, the wild geese fly north and the first rainbows appear."

Motlale slips from Theon's lap. He moves unsteadily to the window. His arm is stretched out behind him, the tube tensed in the pale sunlight irradiating the fluid inside. The boy speaks in Sotho, shaking his head. Daniel looks quizzically at Theon, who once again translates: "But where are all these things you talk about?" the boy says. "The birds and the rain and the mist and the bugs and the bears and the flowers. And the fish! All I see out there are big, big houses."

Theon translates his own reply for Daniel: "Those things are far away, where we can't see, but if we talk about them often enough, again and again, then we see them after all."

The boy shakes his head, looking out at the turbid sky. "It's not there," says Motlale, as channelled by Theon. "It's just in the words."

"How do you manage to translate the English descriptions of Japanese phenomena into Sotho?" Daniel asks in a muted voice.

"I struggle. I can't always find the right words. Sometimes I replace the names of, for instance, plants or birds with things from the Free State . . . "

Yoshikawa drops by, sits down as before in the corner with Daniel and Theon. So far everything is going according to plan with the treatment, he informs them. There is nothing unforeseen. And he thinks the boy is managing well on an emotional level, considering how unfamiliar he must find everything, compared with the simple world he comes from.

"I don't know if 'simple' is the word," says Theon, frowning.

"Forgive me," says the doctor, performing two little staccato head-bows. "My English is not up to standard. I do not mean to insult anybody. All I mean is that Japan is far from the African continent." His feet shift uncomfortably. "May I ask: Have you yourselves been to this city before? Have you visited any of the sights since your arrival?"

"We mainly keep to the immediate area," Theon says. His eyes dart in Motlale's direction. "We want to stay close to him."

The doctor nods politely, turns to Daniel. "And what have you seen so far?"

"Not enough," says Daniel. "I'm actually planning to write an article. For a British paper. On architecture in Tokyo. I must confess I'm still looking for an angle."

"Ah!" says the oncologist, ceasing his shifting about. "The complicated relationship between buildings and people!" He nods as he speaks, his head in irregular conjunction with his speech. "There are many secrets locked up in that. When I first came to Tokyo, after losing my family, I was so caught up in my own grief that I could work no longer. My eyesight started deteriorating badly. Everything was increasingly out of focus."

Motlale has grown calmer. He sits quietly singing, an endlessly repetitive tune.

"I went to see an ophthalmologist colleague," the doctor continues. "He did the standard tests, couldn't find anything wrong. He suggested that I see a psychiatrist."

Motlale has stopped singing, apparently also listening. Outside a siren can be heard.

"Instead of making an appointment with a psychiatrist, I took a week off work. For the first time in many years. I booked a tour here in Tokyo. One concentrating on people living in unusual spaces. For instance, we visited a man living in the narrowest house in the city—just one and a half metres wide. And then a cleaner whose windowless flat leads directly into a supermarket, where he polishes the floors at night. For recreation, when he's done, he goes for a walk, in clean socks down the empty aisles, among all the brightly lit products."

A little smile plays on Doctor Yoshikawa's lips as he talks. It appears and fades at random, Daniel thinks, unconnected to what he's saying.

"Then we visited a young girl, a prostitute, living in a 24-hour internet café—"

"Hang on," Theon says to the doctor. Motlale has signalled to him. He gets up, goes to talk to the boy in a low voice. The boy nods. "He has to visit the bathroom," Theon tells the doctor. The doctor presses a button, summoning the nurse; she detaches the bag. Motlale expels a sudden breath, as if he's been holding it up to now. The nurse and Theon accompany the boy into the corridor.

Doctor Yoshikawa now focuses intently on Daniel. "On the architecture tour we also visited the Nakagin Capsule Tower. It's a futuristic building from the seventies, with residential capsules bolted to a concrete core. Originally built as a place for businessmen having to overnight in the city. Now it's a semi-ruin. Like a rusted spaceship. There are just a few capsules where residents linger on."

The doctor checks his watch. "You should go and have a look," he says. "It may give you ideas for your article. Anyway. You didn't come to sit and listen to me. And I have to go and complete my ward rounds. So let me conclude. In the days after the architectural tour I started to feel better, the sorrow slowly seeping out of my body. And my eyes started to focus sharply again. Light gradually returned. I could work again, try to save patients. Stay busy, be on the go."

Theon and Motlale return. The boy's face contorts when the nurse reconnects him to the tube.

"What I can say about my experience," the doctor says to Daniel, "is that we will never be able to measure the power of the human psyche. And that melancholy, if it's not controlled, can make you blind. But there are also, I've learned, unexpected ways of dealing with obstinate grief." He pauses for a moment. "I wish you the best with your article. I hope you find truth." He gets up abruptly. His little bow is barely visible. He leaves the room.

Theon shakes his head. "Not sure what to make of Yoshikawa. I just hope he's up to the job."

When Motlale's bag of fluid has drained, Daniel and Theon wheel him back to his room. He'd prefer to walk, but he's too feeble, and it's far. When he's back in his bed, two Japanese boys in hospital gowns peep around the door. "Konnichiwa!" they call in unison. Motlale's face brightens. He waves weakly. It's clearly not his first interaction with them. Perhaps the boy's hours here—his days and evenings—are not as dull as one would imagine.

When the two children have left, Motlale closes his eyes and sinks back onto the mattress. He is profoundly exhausted, Daniel can see. Somewhere in the deep tissue the medicine is doing its cruel work.

In the taxi back to the hotel, Daniel and his cousin are

silent for a long time. "If only he could go home healthy," Theon says at last. "Then everything will have been worthwhile. If not, Malefu will never forgive me."

Daniel has made no further attempt to explore ideas around his essay. And his first solo excursion is not to see a building, but to visit an exhibition of an artist recommended by his contact at *The Observer*. Kishio Suga. The exhibition is in a small gallery in Shibuya, high up in a building. Daniel struggles to find the street-level entrance with his GPS. There is construction everywhere around him, gigantic new buildings springing up. The spot indicating his position on the phone's digital map flits around like a phantom. He walks with the device above his head, trying to connect with a satellite in the midst of all the concrete.

At last he finds the entrance. He takes a lift, two dozen floors up, to the gallery. There are videos of Suga's performances from the sixties and seventies. In each of them he seems to be constructing something, working to bring something into being. He is constantly occupied with some kind of object or material, and with labour or something related to it. He potters, is *busy*. He marks and measures and fits and folds and binds and saws and glues and shifts and stacks and packs and cuts. It looks as if he's doing something meaningful, with some purpose in mind. He is not compulsive, systematic rather, and focused. He always works on his own, following meticulous processes, in a punctilious manner, with considerable energy. And yet: Nothing is created. No structure takes shape. Everything is unmade even as it is executed. Everything begins and ends in zero.

It's Motlale's fourth administration of the intravenous medication. Theon has brought him a toy, a scale model of a

Japanese bullet train. The boy doesn't take much notice of it, just watches it askance. He is calmer this time. Perhaps just too tired and weak to resist. Theon sits with the boy on his lap while the nurse is inserting the needle. Motlale frowns, averts his face but doesn't recoil. Daniel can see that he's losing weight; his legs seem as thin as broomsticks.

The doctor comes to check on him again. Everything is still on course with the treatment, he says. The enervation is an unavoidable side-effect. He does not linger to chit-chat, leaves to complete his ward rounds.

Today Daniel's throat feels constricted in this room dedicated to the infusion of poisonous chemicals into veins. There is something evil in the sparkling-clean walls, in the paint and rugs and the chairs they sit on. He excuses himself, leaving Theon on his own with the boy.

He leaves the hospital, making his way to the Hama-rikyū Gardens, where he circles one of the ponds. The dead wings of butterflies and moths quiver on the water, as if whole swarms drowned themselves just to make this moment, this scene, possible. He thinks back to the exhibition he saw yesterday. What is it that you are afraid of, he wants to ask the artist. What are you trying to escape from or ward off? Slowly ideas for his essay start to take shape in his mind. His theme, he now knows, is man-made structures and loneliness. He sits down on a bench, closing his eyes, emptying his mind. He thinks of nothing but the water in front of him. He feels the wind on his cheeks, listens to the most distant sounds.

He opens his eyes. His essay will be titled "Architecture and Death."

Dusk. Daniel and Theon are on their way to a karaoke bar in Ginza. It was Theon's idea. By this time, Daniel has had enough of the city's overdose of light. But his cousin has an appetite for bustle and hubbub. Theon is like a child, experiencing Tokyo as a gigantic toyshop. They hop from one place to another. It's as if, in absorbing new impressions, Theon is starting to fill some of his voids. He evidently feels less of a need to talk, more of a need to see. All these things are helping his cousin, Daniel hopes, to turn away from the subjects he touched on over a plate of ramen soon after their arrival. And from Motlale's pain. They no longer have awkward or personal conversations. Theon speaks only of their daily experiences in the city, new things that mask the internal malaise. The place they're heading for now is the biggest karaoke bar in the world. Daniel looked away and rolled his eyes when Theon proposed it. This is not the first time Daniel has discovered that the longer you travel with somebody, the more obvious your incompatibilities become.

And yet he accompanies his cousin. Perhaps he'll find inspiration in unexpected places for his as yet vaguely outlined essay. They're walking, as always, with Google Maps open on a phone. The blue line tracing the proposed route keeps hopping between streets, repositioning. Theon taps the screen with his finger.

Daniel shakes his head. "Must be a Free State phone." His cousin doesn't laugh, just raises an eyebrow.

At length they find the narrow, tall building and enter. On the ground floor there is a small stage and a modest crowd milling about. Right now, nobody is singing in front of the large video screen. They ascend the staircase. On the next floor there is a corridor with individual studios. They go up another floor. Everything is bathed in cold blue or purple or green light. The floors are of steel. Feet clatter up and down the staircase. The corridors on each level are identical. Theon wants to explore all the floors, even though there's hardly anything to be heard and everything looks the same. People are lounging about on white vinyl sofas, waiting for cubicles to become available. Ten floors, Daniel thinks, and still it's not enough. Each voice is trapped in a soundproof cabin. Only occasionally, as a door opens or closes, can a snatch of a song be heard.

They take a lift down from the top floor. On the ground floor, someone is now onstage, singing a sentimental song. A teenage Japanese boy, slender and shapeless, with a face that Daniel won't recognise in five minutes' time. Theon stops dead, listening. Daniel lifts a hand to take his cousin by the shoulder. It's time to leave. In the light from the stage, he notes to his surprise that there are tears on Theon's face. My cousin, Daniel thinks, is racked with regret over a wasted life. And with all sorts of sorrows and furies. Perhaps with unforeseen erotic urgings. This is Theon's season of remorse and self-pity. Daniel doesn't touch him, lowers his hand.

Daniel now also watches the young singer, ventures deeper into the nebula of sound. He is singing in Japanese, a local song rather than Western pop. And there's something hypnotic about him. His voice is as pure and anxious as a child's in distress. Daniel walks straight up to him, his cousin now forgotten. As he and the boy look into each other's eyes, he wonders what it would sound like if you combined all the voices in all the little studios of this building. If you threw open all the doors on all the floors at once. He thinks of the caterwauling that would arise, a lament projecting Tokyo's pain up far beyond the city's arc of light.

It is four o'clock in the morning when the hotel phone on the pedestal between Daniel and Theon's beds rings. Theon answers. It is Doctor Yoshikawa. Theon switches to speakerphone. The doctor explains in his low voice that he has been called to the hospital, that Motlale has had a serious reaction to the previous afternoon's infusion of medicine.

"How serious?" Theon demands. "What's wrong with him?"

The doctor hesitates for a moment. "I'm afraid it is very serious. I suggest that you come here straight away."

They get dressed and take a taxi. The doctor is awaiting them in the hospital's reception area. He takes them into a small waiting room. His face is drawn. "I have to inform you that Motlale is on life-support machines."

Theon's head rears back violently. "What?! What do you mean? How is that possible? What will you do now?"

The doctor says nothing, lowers his head.

"No," Theon says. "No." He shakes his head. "Please. There must be something you can do."

The doctor looks up. His eyes are small and black, unexpectedly hard. "You are begging now. It's no use being a supplicant." Daniel is surprised that the Japanese man knows this English word, and also at its inappropriate application. He's taken aback by the new tone. Doctor Yoshikawa looks down again, his voice growing softer once more. "I'm afraid nothing further can be done." The doctor performs his little staccato bows. The muscles in his jaw tense up, revealing each individual sinew.

"But—"

Daniel holds up a hand to silence Theon. "Could you please explain what happened, Doctor?"

Yoshikawa turns to Daniel. "I can't say what caused this turn. The natural remedies we combine with the chemotherapy are new and experimental. There is, as you are aware, not a long history of their medical use. There was, among other complications, anaphylaxis—possibly an allergic reaction."

Theon steps forward, too close to Yoshikawa, who draws back his head. "But he's had the same substances three times before!"

The doctor takes a step back. "The effect may be cumulative. We don't have answers yet. There will be a thorough autopsy. And eventually you will have access to the full toxicological report."

Theon swivels around, away from the doctor, throwing up his hands. He exclaims: "Autopsy? What are you saying?"

"I am sorry," Yoshikawa says. "I am so sorry." He nods, nods again. "I'm getting ahead of myself. It is true, though, that the patient is braindead. The organs are still functioning, but there is no prospect of improvement or recovery. I am so sorry."

Theon turns back to Yoshikawa as if he's about to assault him. "Before, you were full of stories about the treatment! Full of promises. All the brochures and photos of sparkling hospital wards and smiling doctors. Now all of a sudden you're not taking any responsibility!"

"I'm sorry," Yoshikawa keeps repeating. "I'm so sorry." He nods and bows slightly. "But, with respect, we made no promises. And the risks were clearly explained. It is experimental—"

"Fuck your experiment!" Theon shouts. He hides his face in his hands, walking to the window.

"You will have to take a decision," the doctor says rapidly and in a low voice to Daniel. "About switching off the machines. You have to decide about that, and fill this in." He hands over a form that he's been holding in one hand.

Theon returns to them in a few long strides, looks at the form in Daniel's hands. "No," Theon says. "No!"

Daniel clasps his cousin's arm, leading him back to the window. Daniel talks calmly to him, trying to soothe him. The doctor slips out.

A nurse conducts them to Motlale, who is now lying in the

intensive care section with an oxygen mask over his nose and a tube in his mouth. Theon stands at the door of the ward; he looks for just a few seconds before turning on his heel and walking away. Daniel follows.

They take a taxi, travelling through the streets while the sun is rising. Halfway back to the hotel, Daniel changes the destination. He takes Theon to the Hama-rikyū Gardens. It is quiet as they walk through the gate. They circle the pond where Daniel wandered before. The water is dark and stagnant. The insect wings that drifted like confetti then have sunk to the bottom or been blown away. Theon rubs his eyes, mussing his hair with both hands. Over and over.

"We have to decide, Theon," says Daniel as they circle the pond a second time. He speaks softly. "Or *you* have to. About switching off the machines. You have a document from Malefu granting you that capacity."

"She had no clue what she was signing." Theon is immediately agitated again. "I want to see the superintendent of the hospital. I want details, I want to know precisely what happened. We may have to start legal proceedings, or at least lay a charge. Perhaps Yoshikawa is a psychopath. Perhaps this is his bizarre way of avenging the death of his own children . . . "

"I think you're going too far now. I don't know exactly what happened, but it did. And formal steps won't gain us anything. You got Malefu to sign all kinds of indemnities because the boy was taking part in medical experiments. You can be sure that they're legally covered."

"But the documents were all in Japanese!"

"Theon . . . " Daniel comes to a standstill, grips his cousin by the shoulders, shakes him gently. "Theon! What is achieved by your anger and frustration? Look, we can set in motion all kinds of proceedings, spend months and years trying to find out what happened here, but it's not going to make any difference."

Theon peers out over the water, at a small wooden structure on the opposite bank, something like a meditation hut with room for only one person. He shakes his head. "To think that some Japanese flower killed him. Of all fucking things."

"We don't know that, Theon. It's not clear what caused his condition."

"I promised her. Malefu. That I would bring him back healed."

That, Daniel wants to say, was not the right promise to make. But he holds his peace.

The machines have been switched off. Motlale's refrigerated body is lying in the hospital's mortuary. Daniel and Theon are sitting in the lounge of the Imperial discussing what to do with it.

"There's no question," Theon says. "We have to fly him out."

"Do you have any idea what that would cost? And do you have an inkling of what's already been spent on this trip, and on hospital expenses? My allowance from my father has stopped until the estate is wound up. I simply don't have the cash flow to cover it all. Let's be realistic: We can have a cremation ceremony. Here in Japan. The two of us. We'll honour him properly, according to Japanese ritual."

Theon shakes his head, compressing his lips, turning away. There is clearly a lot he wants to say. But apparently he's checked by the fact that he can't afford to have the body transported himself.

Later, when Theon has gone for a walk in the streets, Daniel phones a crematorium. There's nobody there whose English is good enough to provide meaningful information and he ends the call none the wiser.

Daniel phones the doctor. The doctor's manner does not suggest in any way that Theon's earlier eruption discomposed him. He explains calmly how the cremation ceremony works. Also how the family members, according to the usual ritual, afterwards pick the uncremated bones from the ash and transfer them to an urn. Daniel thanks him, ends the call.

Daniel tells Theon nothing of this. It would upset him profoundly. Daniel himself can't get past the image of picking the bones from the ash. That aspect they would probably be able to avoid. And yet. He has to admit he has no clue what Basotho burial ritual would entail, but it's sure to be far removed from this kind of procedure. He can't inflict that on Motlale's family in the Free State. Nor on his cousin.

He calls his medical insurance provider in Britain. They refer him to a specialist firm in Japan. He phones them; somebody itemises, in passable English, the costs to fly out the body. It exceeds Daniel's slender remaining cash reserves by a wide margin. For the sake of immediate funds, he decides, he'll increase his mortgage in London. That will bridge the gap until he receives his inheritance. And he might as well put his flat in Cape Town on the market. He has no more use for it. He says nothing of these plans to Theon.

It's their last afternoon in Tokyo. They walk to the Capsule Tower—the one place in the city Daniel wants to see before leaving. Theon wasn't keen, but seemed reluctant to remain behind on his own in the hotel room. He lags slightly behind Daniel.

They stand still, gazing up at the grey residential capsules. Daniel has read that the individual cabins can be unscrewed and bolted somewhere else onto the core, that the entire structure's configuration can be adjusted according to preference.

"Like petals on a stem," Theon says. His cousin is still under the influence of his obsession with seasonal change, Daniel thinks. For his part, he thinks it looks like a satellite with a bunch of crates hanging off it—one that's been jolted out of its orbit and is drifting ever further away. A lonely wreck. Space junk.

Daniel tilts his head back further, holding his hand over his eyes against the light. It is impossible, he thinks, to figure out the pattern of vacancy and occupancy from outside, to say which cells are disused and which accommodate beating hearts. "A few days ago," he says, "I came across a Japanese word. In a catalogue description of the work of Kishio Suga. Looking up at this building, the word comes back to me: 'Kodokusi.' It means 'to die alone and unnoticed.'"

Theon narrows his eyes. He repeats it, slowly, syllable by syllable. "Ko-do-ku-si."

As Theon stands there, the tears start flowing. Daniel comes closer, puts an arm around his shoulders. Around his half-destroyed cousin.

The day they fly out of Tokyo, it starts raining. Without cease, an endless persistence of water from the murky sky.

"Motlalepule," Theon says pensively, looking out of the cabin window as they take off—addressing not Daniel but some abstract audience. "The name means 'the rainmaker.'"

Daniel does not want to return to the farm. He does not feel up to the unavoidable confrontation with Malefu. She would blame him equally for the fact that her son did not come home. He and Theon say goodbye somewhat stiffly at the airport, from where Daniel will travel on to Cape Town. Theon undertakes to return his cousin's rented car, which has been parked on the farm for weeks, to Bloemfontein.

Daniel has still not said a word to his cousin about the various measures he's had to employ to acquire funds. After a few weeks in Cape Town he starts packing up his flat. It sells within days of Daniel putting it on the market; soon he'll be without a home in South Africa. It's the right time to surrender his place here—over the last few years he's become increasingly reluctant to return to Cape Town. And even though he's always travelled here in spite of his father's presence rather than to see him, the old man's death has at last allowed him to bid farewell to the city.

He still hasn't started work on the Japan piece for *The Observer*. And the last few months have also made him abandon—irrevocably, he feels—his attempts to write fiction. They were, in any event, never much more than the mutterings of a boy's voice in a soundproof room. And now that room has imploded.

* * *

Daniel and his cousin haven't been in touch in six months. In the meantime, he's sold his London flat as well. He received an offer sooner than expected on that, too; it caught him unawares. He bought a home outside the city, in Kent, one of the first places an agent showed him, and moved in. And the inheritance arrived, again sooner than anticipated. His sister had evidently seen to it that the winding up of the estate was effected with maximum efficiency and dispatch.

He writes a letter to Theon. An old-fashioned one, which he types on his computer and will print out to send by post. *I'm writing you just a short letter*, he starts. He hesitates, his fingers hovering over the keyboard. There are things he wants to say, about their time together on the farm and in Tokyo. Something holds him back. Those long years when he didn't know his cousin—forgot all about him—once again descend like a heavy curtain. It smothers the words, leaving a blank page before Daniel, space to fill with news. He has, he now tells Theon for the first time, sold his flat in London, as well as the one in Cape Town, and settled permanently in the real England—in the country, in an eighteenth-century cottage with an Aga stove in the kitchen and an open hearth in the living room. It is in Kent—more or less within reach of London, he thought, but he's never been back to the city. He's renounced the life of relationships. He's on his own, in control of his emotional graph. He has a vegetable garden and is, believe it or not, considering acquiring a dog. He even goes to sit in the village pub in the evenings with a warm beer in front of him. He drinks it slowly, before going home to crawl between his cold sheets, read for a while and go to sleep. He travels only occasionally. His wandering days are finally over, he's decided, but he doesn't keep strictly to that resolve. When he does go somewhere, it's nearby, in the northern hemisphere. Actually only the continent.

Sometimes, he writes to his cousin, his new mode of existence makes him shake his head. It's a kind of ironic play on a real life. A pastiche. He deletes "pastiche." It's perhaps not a word his cousin would recognise. Then he retypes it. It feels, he continues, as if he's floating about in a sort of transparent bubble, or trapped in a block of ice. As if nothing can touch him, nothing can impress, move or surprise him. As if he's not actually *seeing*. And yes, he's still staying in the Imperial Hotels of the world. He realises he's never told Theon about this ritual, his cousin won't understand the allusion, but he doesn't delete it.

He starts rereading the letter, realising it's not the brief missive he promised in the first sentence. Halfway through he stops, prints it out. He writes his name at the end in ink, folds it into an envelope, puts a stamp on it. He walks to the post office. It's quite a distance; his cottage is at the edge of the village.

He thinks, as he often does, of the time with his cousin, of the stay on the farm as well as the alienating sojourn in Tokyo. He feels vaguely sorrowful about Motlale, although, if he were to examine his emotions honestly, his grief is really for his cousin's grief. After all, he hardly knew the boy. And he still puzzles over his father's motives for the condition in the will. Had his father nursed the notion that they belonged together, the two cousins, was he attempting to provide Daniel finally with a feeling of home or roots or connection? Daniel smiles, shaking his head. He can't believe that he's so forbearing, that he can construct for his father such nuanced and humane motivations.

What Daniel does not write in the letter is that yesterday he instructed the lawyer by email to pay out half his inheritance to Theon. What's left for himself is more than he could spend in his lifetime. The lawyer has instructions to contact Theon and make arrangements. Daniel phoned his sister last night and mentioned it to her.

"Are you out of your mind?" was her reaction. "Do you have any idea how many decades it took our father to amass all that capital? Do you know what kind of dedication it takes? You could have given it to my children."

How would you know how much dedication anything takes, he wanted to say. Your prosperity is all derived from your husband. And your children have too much as it is. He put down the phone. What had possessed him to phone her? Is the gentle country air softening his brain? Had he forgotten that monetary matters are all that can arouse something like passion in his sister? Had he expected her to praise him for his familial piety? That his generosity with money he hadn't earned would alter her attitude to him?

As Daniel approaches the post office, he slows down. He stops, looks down at the letter and smiles wryly. He's been back in the UK for too long, he realises. He's forgotten how unlikely it is that a physical letter will in fact find its way via some sort of postal service to the godforsaken depths of the Free State. So much for his attempt at slowness, at old-fashioned communication. He sits down on a bench on the village green, tears open the envelope, photographs the pages of the letter with his phone and sends the images electronically to Theon.

Initially there is no reply. Four weeks later, to his surprise, Daniel receives a handwritten letter from Theon by post. All the way from the Free State. He is very grateful for the gesture of gifting him such a large sum, his cousin writes. He was unsure whether he should accept it, but the lawyer persuaded him that Daniel would be left with enough. It was so unexpected, and would make so many things possible. He will have the homestead renovated and improved, erect new fences, fix cribs and pumps. It is for the benefit of his former labourers—he has in the last months handed over the farm to Malefu and her husband. Title has been formally transferred. He himself had made plans to move to Cape Town. He'd had to consider how he could afford it. He'd found a place for a decent rent, was planning to leave in a month's time. He'd thought he'd find an odd job in Cape Town. In the ticket office of a small film theatre. Or in a bookshop. Something like that. Something far removed from his life on the farm. Now, with this windfall, everything was so much simpler. Still, he cherishes no illusions that the move to that dismal city with its grey waves and smell of rotting kelp is going to change his life fundamentally. He knows that it won't entail excitement and glamour, that he will probably feel lonely at times. *I made all my arrangements, I must now confess, on the assumption— the hope—that you would be there. At least at odd times. That*

I could look you up when the place got too miserable. Your letter—the fact that you'd sold up in Cape Town and are now living permanently in the British countryside—was a surprise. Perhaps, he writes, he will now go back to the farm more frequently, will from time to time stay with Malefu and the rest, that's if they'll tolerate him on their property. And who knows, perhaps he'll meet people in Cape Town, perhaps there is someone with whom he can have breakfast in the morning or go to the Karoo for a weekend. But it's probably more likely that he'll end up doing these things on his own. That would also be fine. He has found a new state of calm. A resignation. *I have emptied myself, one could say. And now I'm awaiting the silence. See, cousin, Japan has left a mark on me after all.*

Last but not least, Theon writes, he had, while clearing the farmhouse for the move, come across a letter. From Daniel's father. He had never, after his own father's death, sorted out the old man's documents or even clothes and personal possessions. Now, for the first time, he had to sift through it all. Among all his father's files he'd found the envelope. He wanted to share the letter with Daniel, it's only a single sheet, and he's enclosing it. Perhaps it would give Daniel some kind of insight into his father's last wish that he should seek out his cousin. Or perhaps it would just make everything even more unfathomable.

Daniel waits a day, unable to decide what to do with the enclosed letter. Late the following evening he returns from the pub. At first he sits in darkness, then switches on a reading lamp and unfolds the sheet of paper. It's weightless, the ink showing through the paper. He flattens it, starts to read.

His father is obviously replying to a letter from Theon's father. The voice in the letter is not unlike the one that Daniel knew.

*

You wrote to me about that evening when you and I drank a few glasses of wine, and about what ensued. As regards your assertions that something inside you has "changed irreversibly," that you want to talk, must see me: I'm asking you kindly to reconsider. No, to come to your senses. It was an error of judgement, the kind that men like us, with the kind of future we're planning—that I'm planning with your own sister—cannot afford. Surely you know that. It was the kind of imbecility that can overcome red-blooded men when they've added a few drops of alcohol to the mix, and find the nearest flesh to lay their hands on.

In a few months' time I'm getting married to your sister. We are going to be brothers-in-law, you and I. What happened can never again be referred to. You must forget that evening, as I have forgotten.

Daniel mostly sits in his garden, reading. He has lost all faith in making up stories. Occasionally he produces a short piece for a newspaper, but only when he's approached and if it's a subject he can research from home. After he failed to deliver his article on architecture in Tokyo, *The Observer* has not asked him again. And such requests are becoming scarcer from all sources. He's getting older. He is alone, to be honest. Utterly solitary. His limbs and his voice are growing stiff and loath. His lips are no longer accustomed to talking. Now and again he sees a friend from his London days, but it's a city that claims one's full attention. Many of his acquaintances in that city have grown distant—once you've left London, you've left it. In South Africa he no longer knows anybody apart from his sister and cousin. And his sister he has no wish to contact, nor she him, evidently. He knows that she sometimes travels to England and Europe, that over the years she has probably stayed in hotels close by without contacting him, that she often neglected even to arrange a lunch with him. He wants to write to Theon about all these things, and also about the decades-old letter, the one that only their fathers had read before, but something holds him back.

Months pass. Daniel does not write to Theon, and gets no word from his cousin. Then, out of the blue, he receives an email. His cousin writes that he has moved back permanently to the farm. *Let me not say too much about Cape Town. Except that it did not come up to expectations.* He has built a place on Eenzaamheid, he writes. A kind of cottage. Malefu had to give permission, and her husband. And it was no simple matter. He is now paying rent to his former labourers. *A suggestion, Daniel: How about you come and stay here in the town, in the Imperial Hotel. A good three-quarters of their rooms are usually unoccupied—you'd certainly be the only permanent resident. It's not the Mount Nelson—the place is going to the dogs. What they're serving in the dining room nowadays I don't know, maybe tinned food. But then we could see each other from time to time.*

What do you say, Daniel? How about it? Where you are it's summer now. Here it's winter, yes, and icy. But it will change again. To your east, much further to the east, it is currently Bōshu, the season of grains and seeds: The praying mantises are hatching, the rotting grass transforming into fireflies, the plums turning yellow. If it had been the opposite season, if the earth were to be turned on its head and Japan suddenly ended up in the southern hemisphere, it would now be Tōji, the winter solstice—then the ginseng would sprout, the antelopes shed their old horns and the wheat germinate under the snow.

When Daniel is living in the hotel, Theon continues, they could get to know each other properly. And before long they might consider buying a modest little farm in the vicinity.

Grow vegetables, perhaps keep a few sheep. They could become self-sustaining, take off their watches and switch off their phones, walk and read and swim naked. They'll feel the humming of the telephone poles with their hands, smell the dust, hear the ice crunching under their soles in the morning. They'll be able to listen to the earth, measure themselves by the seasons. And they won't even notice that they are growing old together. To each, the eyes of the other will always be the eyes of a boy.

What do you say to that, Daniel? he repeats. *How about it?*

Daniel looks up from the screen. What to make of this? How to interpret his cousin? And how do you reply to something like this? He can still not figure out what Theon wants, what he desires.

He goes out. For a while he sits motionless in his English garden. It's a mellow, sunny day. The branches of the weeping willow above his head sway lightly. Seeds and pollen drift in the sunlight. He closes his eyes, listens to the silence for a long time. The kind of silence that represents a total absence of life. If he were to ignore the glare of the sun penetrating his eyelids, he could imagine himself in outer space.

He gets up, walks to the village. He goes into the pub, nods at two old men sitting at separate tables, each with a pint of beer. He fetches a beer for himself at the counter, also sits down on his own and drinks as slowly as possible. When he's done, he pushes the glass away, wiping his mouth.

He walks back in the gathering dusk, past the church and churchyard, past the village green and post office. He listens. For the sound of a man or a child. A lamb, an owl, a cricket. Anything. The silence is absolute. The whole village vanishes, slips away into darkness. To fill the silence, he dreams up images of a black wave washing soundlessly over a Japanese village.

Reaching home, he welcomes the sound of the key in the eighteenth century lock of his front door. Without switching on a light, he sits down in the chair in which he always does his reading and writing. He picks up his laptop. He searches Google for images of the term "kleilat." He hardly looks at the pictures of boys on muddy riverbanks that appear. He sits like that until the screen automatically dims and goes to sleep. He listens to the darkness for a while. Then he wakes up his computer and books a one-way ticket to South Africa.

4.
THE BIRTH PAINS OF TERMITES

Hein doesn't know why he's sitting in on this conversation. He hasn't said a word, has become invisible to the other three. Daniel and Theon haven't even introduced him to the social worker. She looks ill at ease, seated across from them. What she's doing, Hein thinks, is trying to establish her authority.

She looks at Theon and says, "To have a child is—"

"War," Daniel interjects. "That's what I'm expecting from the powers that be: non-stop war." He says it in Afrikaans, which she doesn't understand. She turns to him, looking pissed off. "Forgive the interruption, Mrs. Molomo," Daniel says in English, raising his hands as if in surrender. "Do carry on."

"To have a child, I was saying, is not a right. Caring for somebody else's child is doing the work of the state, under the supervision of the state. And you have to understand trauma, and its effect on a child's development." She sounds like a student reading from a textbook, Hein thinks.

Hein can see that Daniel's getting irritated again. He doesn't look at her when he speaks: "It's not clear to me what you mean. We know this child, his history. He's barely three months old. And he's not traumatised. Malnourished, perhaps, but otherwise okay." The social worker frowns, flipping through her file. Daniel continues: "This is his home, this farm. He was born here, has never been away. It's the best place for him. And we are ready and willing to care for him. On a temporary footing, if need be, initially. Eventually, we hope, permanently."

She looks up from her file. "What is your relationship with the child's late grandmother? And what right do you have to occupy this land?"

Theon smiles wryly, looking at Daniel. The social worker's frown deepens. "We were living here by the grace of the deceased owners," Daniel says. "We're bywoners." Daniel's voice is ironic, close to laughter. The social worker eyes him severely, makes a note. Hein is surprised that she doesn't enquire into the relationship between Daniel and Theon.

Hein has been living with Daniel and Theon for five months now. Next to their cottage, in an outside room that probably used to be a store or a worker's accommodation. A squatter in a squatter's yard, as Shelley said before clearing out. And Hein knows the whole history. The baby has been with Daniel and Theon in their cottage for the past month. This social worker is new on the scene. She looks green— too young, out of her depth. The child was born when Hein had been on the farm for something like a month. The baby initially lived in the main house. With an old sick woman, Malefu was her name. The baby was her grandchild, the son of her daughter. He was born there in that house, the boy, barely fifty metres from the cottage. Daniel had told Malefu again and again to call them immediately when the child arrived—they would get medical assistance or take her daughter to hospital in the bakkie. But Daniel and Theon were kept in the dark till the next morning. When it was too late. By then the young mother was dead. Apparently during the night Malefu had called someone herself from the township, some kind of traditional midwife. Who vanished when the sun rose and the young woman was lying on the kitchen floor in her own blood. Hein didn't see it himself, Daniel told him.

They could even have called a helicopter, Daniel said; he and Theon were signed up for that kind of medical emergency.

So then Malefu cared for her grandchild for the first two months. She was old and feeble, her husband even older and feebler. They were now the only two people in that rambling house. Their other children had left for the city a long time ago, Daniel told Hein. Only the daughter had stayed. Daniel and Theon wanted to look after the baby here in their own cottage, but Malefu wouldn't hear of it. Daniel and Theon bought baby formula. And a cot, and bedding, and nappies. They pleaded, explained to Malefu that she was old, that they could help. Could take charge. She refused, fought like a tigress. So Daniel and Theon took all the baby stuff and left it for her there in the farmhouse. And that's probably okay, Hein thought. After all, the child didn't belong to them.

But Daniel called in Social Services, trying to have the child taken away. Hein was on the scene when the first social worker turned up, and sat in the same chair Missus Molomo is sitting in now.

"Malefu can't care for him properly," Daniel told social worker number one. "Look at the state of things in that house. She's sick, she moves with difficulty. As it is she has to look after her bedridden husband. And she's uninformed, the child is underweight. When it's quiet at night, we can hear him crying—screaming. We'll raise the child here with us. With great care. We have financial resources. And all the time in the world. It's a minute's walk away from his grandmother. She can see him every day. As often as she likes."

Social worker number one went straight from Daniel and Theon's cottage to the main house, which, to be honest, wasn't exactly clean and neat. The social worker made her decision: Daniel and Theon had no right to the child. He had to stay with his grandmother. Social Services would monitor the situation. She could find no evidence of neglect, she said. And even if she had, the child couldn't just go and live with Daniel and Theon, he'd have to be looked after by the state. Or by relatives. There are laws, she said. And processes. We don't just hand out children like presents.

Three weeks later, Malefu's husband died. And a week later, so did she. In her bed in the farmhouse, with the child in her arms. It was Hein who heard the baby crying in the night. Hysterically, non-stop. It was he, Hein, who sprinted to the cottage to wake up Daniel and Theon. They both ran to the farmhouse. Hein followed, slowing and then stopping some distance from the house, waiting. Daniel emerged with the baby in his arms, without a word. The next day he told Hein that Malefu had been cold already. And she'd clung on. They'd struggled to get the child out of her arms.

Since then the child has been staying here with them, with Daniel and Theon. They'd informed Social Services—otherwise they could be accused of child snatching—and four weeks later, this woman turned up. She's looking down now, paging through her papers as if searching for answers, arguments for taking the child with her rather than leaving him here in this house of white men. Where she obviously can't figure out who's who or what's going on. Seems she can't find a good enough reason. She shuts her file decisively.

"For the time being we'll leave the child in your care," she says. "But I'll be back. We're going to track down the family members. Uncles or aunts. Cousins. Somebody will come to fetch the baby."

Hein knows that Theon has a number for Malefu's older daughter, who lives in Joburg. She was here for her sister's funeral, the only one of the children who turned up. She wasn't here for her father's burial, and it seems she doesn't know that Malefu has died. Daniel and Theon had to decide, after Malefu's death, whether to phone her or Social Services about the child.

Now Theon says: "I'm afraid I don't have contact details for any family members. They haven't been here for a very long time."

The social worker puts both hands on her file, looking at Theon. "Not even for their mother's funeral?"

"No."

"So, when last?"

He thinks for a while. "Perhaps two or three years ago."

The woman doesn't seem satisfied. "Remember," she says, looking from Theon to Daniel and back again, "I can make a return visit at any time, come and inspect what's going on here. Without warning. *Any* time."

Hein reckons she's trying to make her eyes look like an eagle's.

Hein goes for a walk, as always, in the late afternoon, when the air has freshened. He looks back at the white cottage, like a tiny boat in an ocean of grass. He thinks of the two men in whose yard he's living. He's never really been able to figure them out. Daniel has told Hein that years ago Theon was the owner of this farm, that he gave it to his labourers. That later he had to ask Malefu if he could come back, come and live here; after all, they went back a long way. Apparently she hadn't agreed right away. Her husband, who'd been one of Theon's labourers for a long time, had to persuade her. So Theon built the white cottage in a spot designated by Malefu. Twelve or thirteen years ago, Theon explained. And later Daniel came to live with him. Just about all the farms around here were later expropriated anyway. Theon had just got in ahead of the government. On the surrounding farms, there are lots of families living on bits of the land. Daniel and Theon say it's not being utilised properly. Hein thinks it's okay. Good old-fashioned capitalism, having to put in extra labour to maximise wealth. Fuck that. The people who grow vegetables for themselves and milk their own cows for their own kids look relaxed to him, happy. Except for the kids who move out later to look for a job in Joburg or Bloemfontein.

But to get back to Daniel and Theon. They look so old to him, and depressed, both of them. He'd put them at about sixty. He's not even sure that they're gay, and he doesn't care. When he was still going to the hotel bar in town, there was this one other white guy still living around here. He left a few weeks ago. Anyways, this guy said that the two were actually cousins. So who knows what's what.

Hein is not so sure about these two as parents. So maybe they're generous—after all, they gave him and Shelley a place to stay. But those two have been fucked up for a long time. They've gone rigid, like sticks. He doesn't think they're an item. They're together in a way but on their own at the same time. As if their separate togetherness is based on some mysterious backstory, on some other person's pain and fucked-upness. As if they're trying to set something straight that somebody else messed up. He doesn't quite know how to put it, but one thing's for sure, they're weird. The social workers are pretty useless, and they obviously have their own ideas and agendas, but speaking for himself, he's also not so sure the two of them should have a child.

Hein spreads his arms as he walks so the grass lining the path caresses his hands. He thinks of Daniel and Theon's way with the baby. It's so clinical, so precise. The two of them wear hospital masks so as not to infect it. Hein hasn't seen this since the time of the pandemic. What must the kid think of aliens like that carting him around everywhere? They feed him milk from fancy bottles that look superfuturistic. And they make him sleep in an extra-wide white cot. It's as if he's being raised in a laboratory. Or like in a sci-fi movie where people have been cryogenically frozen. Outside there's white grass and silence; inside, white sheets and silence. And the smell of Dettol and alcohol. Everything sterilised. Hein is not allowed to touch the baby. They're okay with him coming to watch TV. But they get uptight if he goes anywhere near the nursery.

Hein takes a short cut through the long grass to the poplar grove. It's cold. Dew chills his open hands. That child is going to waste away from not being touched enough, he thinks. The baby's skin, he reckons, will grow hungry. Somebody should rub his skin. Maybe not with fat, like the local people use, but something rich and shiny. A few germs are good for babies, that's what he believes. Just think of all they're exposed to in the process of natural birth. And of the women around here who rub cattle dung on the umbilical cords of the new babies. The child needs a noisy environment, where he can start enjoying the pleasures of life. Where somebody will give him honey and brown sugar in his bottle and hold him all day. And he deserves a bed where he doesn't have to stretch out his arms and wave them like windmills to find the limits of this huge new world. It's as if he's drifting in outer space. What he needs, Hein thinks, is the smell of soil and grass and armpits. Real warm breath. The sounds of life.

The baby doesn't have a name. Or rather, Malefu refused to tell Daniel or Theon his name. Ditto for Social Services—on the social worker's file there's just a surname. Now his real name is buried forever in Malefu's dead, secret throat. Now he's just "the baby." He has to be given a new name. One that fits exactly, that will balance on top of his old name like a wooden block placed on another one by a child.

Hein sits down in the poplar grove. There's a trickle of

cold water in the spruit. He tugs the sleeves of his jersey down over his hands. He and Shelley used to come and sit here sometimes, in the beginning. Shelley, he thinks, shaking his head. He can't believe she's gone. Even though he doesn't really want to, he thinks back to their first meeting. At a music festival, of course. Hein already had years and years of rock concerts and festivals under his belt. After he dropped out of engineering at age nineteen, he started playing in bands. He didn't want to play hard guitar rock like every other Afrikaans band. He wanted to do something more electronic, more ambient, to experiment with rap and beatboxing, that kind of stuff, but his mates, who were mainly still at university, just wanted to do the standard heavy numbers. He had no choice, he had to fit in. Guitar and synths. Sometimes percussion, but that wasn't his strong suit. They did a whole bunch of smaller events to start. Dumps like Kimberley and Paarl. Student gigs, pubs in Bloemfontein and Pretoria. Then Rocking the Daisies, Oppikoppi. Hein was hooked. He was at every festival, from the first set to the last. If he wasn't performing he was in the audience. He liked electro bands as well, did Ultra every year. And blew his mind at AfrikaBurn. He didn't need much—his tent, petrol for his fucked-up Nissan bakkie, basic food, beer. His shoes he made himself. In-between he slept on the sofas of friends, guys who'd been students with him, old pals from his school days in PE. To make a bit of money in-between he had a market stall. He worked with leather—sandals, wallets, that kind of stuff. He didn't make much, leatherwork was kind of old news.

The bands didn't really work out. The other guys saw it as a stopgap, something to do before carrying on with their real lives. Later Hein dropped the music-making, mainly just running his stall at festivals and flea markets, helping out here and there with synths and stuff. Next thing he knew, he was in his thirties, still hanging out with younger guys and chicks, drinking beer in the dust. He's not an idiot. He could see they were just tolerating him, mocking him behind his back. In their world thirty is middle-aged, thirty-five ancient. He knew he had to move on.

He waited for inspiration on what to do next. He wanted to do one more Rocking the Daisies. And there, under the open skies, he met Shelley. She was a fresh breath, a cool breeze. When he spotted her at a set of one of his favourite bands, she took his breath away. She was in a kind of trance, eyes shut, head thrown back. She was obviously blown away by the energy on stage. The line of her forehead, nose and lips—the proud, vulnerable neck!—made his heart beat faster. He scraped up courage, edging closer through the moshing crowd. She was just about next to the stage.

Hein leant over, shouting at her: "How about this band? Aren't they befok?" She said nothing, just smiled sweetly, turned her face even further towards the clouds, ponytail swinging. "This is my life," Hein said, his mouth to her ear. "This is how I exist: from song to song."

When she opened her eyes, they were the colour of the sky suspended over them like an upside-down ocean. "Me too," she said. "Five minutes at a time. Just as long as the music lasts." She was probably on something. Her blood was pulsing with love and her cheeks were soft. But he believed her. She danced backwards into his arms; her ponytail teased his face.

"I deny suffering and death," he shouted. "At this moment they don't exist."

She laughed. The laugh was challenging, but not humiliating. "What are you on about?"

"In the music there's no pain, girl, only ecstasy."

"You only exist for me as long as the music lasts," she said. "As long as they're going crazy onstage and my hands are in the air." He said nothing more. Standing behind her, he just took her arms and held them up, her index fingers now pointing heavenward.

A few songs later he led her away by the hand. And he did, as it turned out, carry on existing for her, even when the music faded away. In his tent they caressed each other while he talked and talked. She didn't say much. But they understood each other. Unlike some of the other girls, she didn't mind that he was older. "You have experience," she said. "You get me." Her head was on his chest, her breath in his neck. "You make me feel safe."

He drank a lot of beer, and she slipped a pill into his mouth. In the early hours he got deep, started talking about things he could share with very few people. Philosophical stuff. Things he'd been thinking about for a long time. Also stuff that just came to him while he was talking.

He stroked her hands, rubbing each one of her fingers. "Everybody thinks," he said, "that hands were developed by evolution to grip tools, or make fires. To fight with a spear or kill animals." He slipped his fingers in between hers. "But they're actually formed to fit into another person's hand. Knuckle to knuckle, joint to joint. And arms? Their main purpose is to bend in the right places so you can hold another person close. They're designed to keep another body against yours . . ."

They lay for long periods without talking, dozing off, waking again, stroking each other some more. She pushed her hands into his hair—long, down to his back. "These fingers are designed to get a grip on your mane," she said drowsily. He smiled in the dark. That was his pride, the hair. A bit fine, like a girl's, but it *grew*. And when he listened to his favourite bands, it spilled down all over his face. Then he didn't brush it away. Then it made him vanish.

For a while they were awake at the same time. Hein lit a lantern and they lay like that, looking at each other. His eyes so close to hers that her pupils were out of focus. Even closer to his eyeball, Hein saw something moving on the floor of the tent. He picked it up carefully: a termite. They turned their heads towards it. "You won't believe how complicated these insects are," Hein said. He wondered if he should carry on, if anybody, even Shelley, could understand his weird interests. Who cares if he embarrasses himself, he thought.

"Do you know Eugène Marais?"

She shrugged. "Does he sing in a band?"

"No, no . . . a writer. Been dead a long time. Wrote among other things a book about termites." He sat up straighter, made his voice serious. "He writes about all the amazing ways in which they function, about how the nest works together as a single body." Hein turned to Shelley, propping up his head with his hand, elbow on the floor. "Like how the termite queen lays eggs. Apparently she makes a lot of weird movements. Swivels her feelers, lifts her abdomen and stuff. And when the eggs have been laid, she turns around and looks at them closely, touches them, then lies down with them. It turns out: She *hurts* when they emerge. She has birth pains."

Shelley's eyes had closed. He wondered whether she was concentrating or drifting off to sleep. He explained how the queen fed the baby termites droplets of liquid when they emerged, snow-white and helpless, in damp little underground gardens. "Marais's point is—only animals that experience birth pains care for their offspring. The young of animals that feel nothing when giving birth have to cope on their own in the world. Marais describes experiments that prove it. For instance, if you drug a sheep while she's lambing, she rejects the lamb." Hein told her how Marais described the gentleness of a scorpion mother. "After the young have emerged, with their pincers and stings and all—after all that pain—she carries them around lovingly on her back . . . "

Shelley's hand was limp in his. She wasn't listening any more. He disentangled his fingers, brushed her hair from her cheek. With his index finger he traced a vein in her neck. They were in the depths of the night. She opened her eyes abruptly and burst into tears. She was coming down. She started telling him how she'd dropped out of her marketing degree a year ago, how angry her parents were, how she just wanted to breathe a bit, discover the world, find her independence, and how Hein was exactly what she needed now. It kind of spoiled the moment, Hein thought, but he placed his hand on her warm stomach and forgave her.

It was a long night. They slept through the next day, bathed in sweat in the zipped-up tent. While the crowd outside kicked up dust and stumbled over tent pegs, while the bands made a racket on stages. It was hot and stuffy and noisy. It was like sleeping in hell, and it was wonderful. Hein woke up in the sweatiest part of the day. Shelley's body was still limp. He touched her with his fingertips and thought of Eugène Marais's test to prove that the termite queen felt pain when she was laying eggs. You take a glass filament, apparently, and dip the tip in acid. And if you touch her with it, you see that her feelers do exactly the same things as when she's pushing out those eggs.

Fast forward. They were basically on the road for two years, he and Shelley. They attended a lot of music festivals (so that hadn't been Hein's last festival after all) and tried to launch a band or two, but it didn't pan out. Let's face it, he wasn't great on the instrumentals, and her singing voice was just too shrill. When they'd just about run out of money—hardly anybody bought leather sandals any more and Shelley only waitressed occasionally—they moved in with her parents. In a garden flat. Her father was not impressed with Hein, and showed it. He couldn't grasp that Hein was a free spirit, that he was on the kind of journey the old man never had the balls even to consider. Hein wasn't prepared to spend his days listening to the man's insults because he didn't have a corporate job or wear a suit. He packed his stuff and left, sleeping in his bakkie for a while. Then he and Shelley went to one last event, a small festival in the Free State with some of their favourite bands. When it was over, while they were on the way to drop her at her parents—Hein had no clue what he was going to do next—his bakkie broke down. They walked to the nearest farm to look for help, and so they came to knock at Daniel and Theon's front door. The two men gave them supper, said they could overnight in the outside room. The nearest garage that could tow the car was in Bloemfontein or Welkom, and they would have to order parts. It could take time.

Except that Hein had no money to have the car fixed. Or rather, what he had left he'd rather use for essentials. To buy food, basically. When Hein asked if they could stay in the outside room for a few weeks in exchange for work, Daniel said yes. Except that it was clear to Hein that there was no work to speak of being done on that farm.

Fast forward another three weeks or so. The silence and the grass and the weirdness of the two men quickly got too much for Shelley. Besides the fact that Hein had no drive—or money—to move on. Even in the bar in town, where Shelley wanted to go in the evenings to escape the silence, they had less and less to say, had to drink more and more just to talk to each other.

On the last evening, they were both more or less blotto when they drove off from the hotel in Daniel and Theon's bakkie. Hein shouldn't really have been driving. On the stretch of dirt road to the farm Shelley yelled at him a few times when he veered into the grass on one side or the other. Back in their room, while Hein was watching Shelley undress, he suddenly felt a silver flame in his breast. It was one of those moments when you just have to let the universe in. He took off all his clothes, went to stand in the doorway, breathing in the cold air, and started running. Into the grass. It swished around him, stroking his body, wetting his cheeks. He ran and ran till his lungs were burning. He stood still, looking up at the moon, listening to the silence. Shelley would follow him, he was sure, she must surely also feel what he was feeling. And her clothes would remain behind in a heap next to his in the room. The grass was too high to see anything, but they'd hear each other, would move swish-swishingly closer until they found each other. Then they'd hold one another and everything would be okay again, they'd never even need to talk again. Hein stood waiting. And waiting. Until his teeth started chattering.

It took him a while to find his way back, the grass was so long and he was a bit lost. And still quite drunk. The bedroom door was closed but not locked. She was asleep. He got into bed naked, waited for the shivering to stop.

"Good night, Shelley." She didn't reply. "Don't you think it's weird how people say 'Good night' and kiss and hug each other before going to sleep? As if the night is a valley or a dark forest or a deep river, and you're hoping the other person will make it to the other side. I hope you'll still be breathing tomorrow morning, Shelley. And me too." She replied with a soft snore.

When Hein woke up with a thick head—the sun was pouring white light into the room—Shelley stood there looking at him. She shook her head and said: "You're lost. You're nowhere."

He sat upright. The light hurt his eyes. "Shit, it's early in the morning for statements like that. So then tell me: Why are you with a loser?"

"I didn't say you were a loser. But you've lost yourself. You don't know who or where you are . . . Anyway, I can't talk to you when you're so defensive."

"Defensive?" He rubbed the sleep from his eyes. "How do you reply to 'lost' and 'nowhere'? That's pretty absolute."

"Hardly. If you're lost you can find your way back."

"And I'm doing that! Finding a way. I'm not washed up. I'm here for a reason. You don't understand my trajectory, don't get my energy any more. I'm on an interior mission, on the way to enlightenment. I'm emptying myself, I'm becoming pure, *present*. I could go to Japan—"

"Well, if you had the money . . . "

"I could go to Japan, but who needs to go poking around in Eastern temples when the whole of the Free State with its ocean of grass is a temple? When you can dissolve yourself here in the silence? I am here to lose the self and find the Self."

She pursed her mouth. "You're here because your car broke down, Hein."

"I'm here with *you*. And I wish you'd join me on the journey. You can't let in the light if you don't empty yourself first. You have to be patient. Just wait, you'll see. The gods will come and find you here in the silence. When the time's right." He looked from Shelley to the window, where the morning sun was so bright that you got only a vague impression of the planet of grass out there. "Sometimes, you know," he continued, "I walk around here and imagine that I'm levitating. Then I see all the footpaths of the Free State slowly flowing together down there. Becoming a network of routes where all those who've been lost, been looking for one another, can find each other again . . . "

Shelley started pacing in the small room. The light was too much for Hein. His girlfriend was out of focus, like in an overexposed photo. He sat up straight, his voice urgent. "Don't you feel it, Shelley? How everything here is as transparent as glass during the day, and at night so frozen and clean . . . and when everything freezes like that outside, then you *fall*. Fall and fall. While you're sleeping you can do things that would kill you when you're awake. You can test the abyss. And it's bliss not knowing what you're going to find down there."

She rolled her eyes, pulling at her hair. "For fuck's sake, Hein! Enough already with this new-age bullshit. You're right. You're not awake, you're sleepwalking. Sleep*falling* anyway. And you're going to hit rock bottom. I don't want to sleep with you above the abyss any longer. Or fall or whatever. We're stuck here in the middle of fucking nowhere. In the crazy grass, in a tiny room. We are *lost*. You're making me just as lost as you. I'm leaving now." There was no need for her to say anything more, but she did anyway. "I'm going to get my life back, Hein. And that doesn't include you."

She packed her rucksack, asked Daniel to take her to a town where she could catch a bus to Joburg. Hein made sure to get out of the way before having to say goodbye. He came to sit in this very poplar grove. It's dusk now, it was broad daylight then. Then, like now, he listened to the silence. Not even the guineafowl made a sound, hovering like ghosts at the edge of the shadows. They're fast asleep overhead now, ignoring him. Then, he examined the tiny imperfections on the trunks of trees, like scars on a lover's body. Now, in the dusk, he can make out only faint blemishes on the poplars, like bruises.

Hein gets to his feet, he is cold and stiff. He leaves the shelter of the trees, walking back slowly. For the last few days he's been having supper with Daniel and Theon. He feels his ribs. He's been eating badly, for years now. Takeaways, or cheap sausages cooked over a fire. Or stuff from tins, heated on a small gas stove. He looks at the white cottage over there in the distance, in the sea of grass still holding on to the last of the sunlight. He senses that he's becoming an irritation to Daniel and Theon. Especially now that the baby without a name is sleeping there. A little prince in the midst of everything. Like a blank sheet of paper lacking even a heading.

He stops next to the old family graveyard. There's a new granite headstone towering over all the old sandstone graves. Malefu's husband and daughter lie buried in the township cemetery, but Daniel and Theon buried her here. Hein was present. The three white men were alone at the graveside. Daniel read something as she was lowered into the ground, a poem. Hein asked him later what it was. Larkin, he said. He copied the words out for Hein, and Hein learned a bit of it by heart. He recites it now in the dusk:

"The trees are coming into leaf
Like something almost being said;
The recent buds relax and spread,
Their greenness is a kind of grief."

He likes it. He's been trying to write songs again, these past few months, and sometimes ideas come to him. But there isn't even one complete song yet. Scraps, but they don't gel into a single tune. Perhaps, he thinks, he should rather try to write poems. The kind of words that stick in your head and keep churning around there.

Hein walks around the graveyard. The graves are black against the dusk. Like a miniature city, this square with its various headstones. It's fenced in with barbed wire. To keep the dead in, or the living out. There are, in any case, gaps everywhere. Something or somebody has escaped already, or invaded the city. A strange glow attracts him to the corner facing Malefu's grave. He squats down, switching on his phone light. It's a smaller grave. The only headstone made of marble. He wipes dust from the letters. A child, he sees. Died when he was ten. *Motlale*, he reads. "You'd have been twenty-five this year, dude," Hein says. "A man. But you were interrupted. Frozen. You'll stay ten forever." For a moment Hein is overtaken by a weird feeling. He's a bit jealous.

Hein closes the door of the cottage gently when he comes in. The baby must be sleeping. He hears Daniel and Theon whispering in the kitchen. He peeks into the nursery. In the dark the nameless child is lying on his back in the cot. He's paddling with his arms as if he's still swimming inside his mother. He's making odd sounds, anxious and excited. He's testing the world, seeing if any echoes return to him.

Daniel has prepared a stew with many kinds of herbs, too many for Hein's liking. Mediterranean, apparently. Daniel thinks he's European, Hein reckons, with all his fancy recipes, weird music and books and art movies. After supper Daniel and Theon go to their bedroom. There's a single bed against each wall, Hein can see that from the living room, even though he's never been inside. Hein will never figure them out, these two. He has, in any case, never seen them touch each other.

There's a huge TV in the cottage. Hein is watching a sci-fi movie he found on Daniel's shelf of DVDs (how retro, Hein thought). He likes the movie's sets, all in grey and blue. Everything is abstract, hazy. The concept of the story is that in the future, emotion is a disease. There's no more sex or relationships, all babies are created in laboratories. All unproductive activities, things intended only for emotional pleasure, are banned. Special police monitor any transgressions. The main character cultivates orchids in secret. The police, acting on a tip-off, discover the greenhouse and destroy it along with everything inside. There's a close-up of a flower being crushed under the heel of a boot. Everything in a sort of blue light. The guy growing the orchids also has a secret girlfriend. There's a scene in which the couple discover that she's pregnant, the orchid being crushed is projected onto their anxious faces . . .

Hein hears voices in the bedroom. He turns down the volume, approaches on tiptoe, presses his ear against the door. Perhaps they're discussing him.

Daniel's talking: " . . . and now that it's time to leave, we're trapped. In a prison of grass. Something like that. I guess it's my punishment. For my fantasy of return, the naïveté of it. And because of daring to want a child . . . "

"I hope I'm not part of the punishment, of your jail without walls."

"Oh come on, Theon. You know very well escape means nothing if it's not with you. As soon as the child—"

"You always just assume that I'll come along."

"And how precious you always are! What feigned insecurity! Let me spell it out again, then: I don't assume you'll come, but *of course* I want you with me when we leave this pitiless country."

There's a moment's silence. Theon says: "Was it really so disastrous? For you to settle in here again, even on new terms?"

Daniel now also sounds subdued. "No, you know how it is. It's just frustration boiling over. About the machinery we're being exposed to now. The challenges that lie ahead. The uncertainty, the waiting."

For a while they say nothing. Theon continues: "Anyway,

the child. If things work out, it all falls away, all this doubt and regret. If only there was a way to get past the dodgy bureaucracy . . . "

"Unless we kidnap him and take him to the UK, no. We'll have to see the procedures through. Or at least start them. Nobody's going to be sympathetic to our cause. At least not the bureaucrats. And the courts, who knows? Times are very different now from when we went to Japan—"

"Please. I can't . . . " A moment's silence. "I ask you, Daniel: What rational creature could believe that an uncle or aunt who doesn't even know the child would make a better parent? Somebody who could offer him nothing but a precarious existence in a Joburg township?"

"You know how the old dynamics always play out here. But let's not forget—there *are* logical things counting against us. Age, for one. In any case, frustration won't get us anywhere. We'll have to fight in the trenches."

"'War,' hey?"

"I grant you, that intervention was a mistake. Heat of the moment. I won't antagonise the social worker again." Daniel hesitates. "And, yes, as a last resort we may have to oil the wheels . . . When in Rome and all that."

They are quiet again. Hein's ear is numb against the door. He turns his head, applies the other ear.

"In the mayhem of the last few weeks," Daniel says, "we haven't even considered the fact that we're squatting on someone else's land. And we've almost certainly overstayed our welcome. If we were ever welcome. We can expect the children here at any moment, ready to toss our furniture out of the cottage."

"And then we can forget about the adoption, even if they tolerate us."

Silence, once more.

"When it's all over . . . " Theon says, "once we're safely seated on an aircraft with him, then we can give him a name."

Daniel speaks slowly. "Then we can give him a name, yes." For a moment the only audible sound is that of the generator outside. "And incidentally, I think we should get married. For administrative convenience. It will make a visa for you easier, perhaps also citizenship for him."

"Hmm, what a romantic way of proposing."

"You know, the older I get, the more I fall back on bare-bones pragmatism. Like my father, once upon a time." They laugh softly. Just for a few seconds. The covert kind of laugh of people who have known each other for a long time. Like a conspiracy. Hein suddenly senses: Things are more complicated, more intimate between these two men than he's realised. He hardly knows them.

"I hear," says Theon, "that there's pressure in the coalition to abolish same-sex marriages."

"Yip. The joys of radical black nationalists as minority partners. Before we know it, adoption rights might go the same way. So, what do you say? You and me? Home Affairs in Bloemfontein? We can celebrate with a glass of champagne at an Imperial Hotel."

"Tricky with a baby, a wedding trip like that."

"Yes," says Daniel. "And it's not as if we can leave him with our lodger." "God, no," says Theon. "And speaking of someone overstaying their welcome . . . "

Hein walks the short distance in the dark to his outside room. Out here the generator sounds very loud. It's become his nocturnal soundtrack, this noise, pounding out the rhythm of his life. Like a thunderstorm that's constantly threatening but never breaking or passing.

He lies down on the cold bed. The generator's hammering

sounds fainter. Sometimes in the evenings he lies like this for hours, looking at the ceiling. After Shelley left, he went to one or two parties on neighbouring farms, things that guys in the hotel bar told him about, to meet girls. Though local girls don't do that much for him. Does that make him a racist? He doesn't think so, he's slept with one or two. And he was, come to think of it, interested in one that he met at the last party, a lovely Sotho girl from Joburg out here to see her family. But if she was ever interested, she cooled down quickly when she realised he wasn't exactly loaded.

The generator cuts out. That means it's half past nine. Hein feels for his battery lamp, clicks it on. He surveys the empty room, just a heap of clothes and a rucksack in the middle. There's nothing left for him here. He has to admit that now. This phase of his life is over. The time of crashing casually on people's sofas or in somebody's outside room. The time of festivals and Shelley and spiritual journeys and flogging sandals at markets, shit like that. He has to figure out the next chapter of his life, move on, give new shape to his existence.

He thinks of Daniel and Theon's conversation, their remarks about him. He thumps the wall with his fist. Do they really think *they* are obvious carers—or parents—for a kid? Fuck them and their emigration schemes. Fuck the money they can take anywhere. Shelley, who'd bonded with them more than he had, said they were loaded, she didn't know why they were staying in this shithole. And now they want to take the kid away to a damp island up north. Hein shakes his head, even though nobody can see it. No, he's from here, that child. And he needs a name from here.

As if the little boy knows what he's thinking, Hein hears him faintly starting to bawl over there in the cottage. He smiles to himself in the dark.

Hein has an early-morning shower. It's an outside shower, behind his bedroom. Beneath his feet there's a concrete slab, a shining stream cascades over his body. The sun is bright but without any heat. The water is so cold it scalds his skin. His hair is longer than ever, all the way down to the middle of his back. He closes the tap, dries himself. Next to him lies an electric shaver. It's not been used for such a long time, he had to put a new battery in this morning. He shaves his head while sunning his bare, skinny body. He rinses off the left-over hair, leaving it there on the concrete. It looks as if somebody's been washed down the drain, leaving just their hair sticking out.

He hangs out in the outside room all day, packing his rucksack in the late afternoon. When he's done he lies down on his bed, thinking back to the times, as a student, he stayed in bed instead of going to class. He remembers how the sounds of buses and cars and people, of everything moving and everyone doing things—with him so totally static, paralysed, as still as death—used to calm him. He wanted to be left behind, wanted to float into nothingness. Now he's in a totally different mode. He's preparing mentally for the mission ahead.

He has supper with Theon and Daniel. Hein had to wait while they fed the baby his formula, mixed with warm water, and put him to bed. And he had to keep his distance. Hein notices the two men checking out his shaved scalp, glancing at each other.

"I like the new style," Theon says, gesturing at Hein's head. "I hardly recognise you."

Maybe that's the big idea, Hein wants to say, but doesn't.

"Why so quiet tonight, Hein?" Daniel asks after a while, soup spoon to his lips.

He shrugs. "I'm just meditating a bit."

After supper Hein says he's going to finish watching the

movie. The other two go to bed early, as always. They close their door. They have a complicated baby monitor that not only tells them what's happening in the nursery, but also sets off an alarm when the baby stops breathing. Or is picked up from his bed.

Hein lets the rest of the movie about lost babies and orchids run. The volume is low so as not to disturb the two men or the sleeping baby. Hein isn't really watching. He's waiting. After a while he mutes the TV and listens. He hears the two men snoring lightly. He goes to stand by their door, opens it a chink. It's too dark to make out anything inside. He pushes the door open further. A faint blue TV light penetrates the room. He walks straight to the monitor on the bedside table next to Daniel and takes it. He tiptoes back, closing the door behind him again. He finds two plastic bags in the kitchen. He enters the nursery—his first time in here—and looks at the sleeping child. His movements are quick and focused. He puts the monitor down. In one bag he packs clothes and nappies, in the other bottles and dummies and formula and medicines and creams. He grabs the stuff in random handfuls, not really knowing what it's all for. The noises he's making echo on the monitor's speaker. The doubling of each sound convinces him he's doing the right thing. He drapes a baby blanket over his shoulder. He fiddles with the monitor, trying to figure out how to switch off the breathing pad. At last he manages it. He takes a deep breath, his heart hammering his ribs. He picks up the little boy from his bed. With his free hand he takes the plastic bags. The child groans gently. Hein tightens his grip, presses the face to his shoulder as he slips out through the front door.

He opens the door to his room. Without switching on the light, he zips the baby inside his jacket, against his chest. He picks up the rucksack where it's waiting for him. He straps himself into it with some effort, clutching the plastic bags in one hand. His other hand is on the child's back. He's groaning again now, half-awakened by the saddling up. Then he starts whining. Hein pats his palm against the baby's back. Tap-tap. Tap-tap. Like a heartbeat. The boy stops grizzling. Then they are out into the dark.

The wind is cold in Hein's face. The vibration of the lorry sends the baby to sleep under his jacket, nice and cosy up against him. He'd rather be in the cab, but the driver shook his head when he pulled up, even though there was a wide stretch of seat next to him.

"But I have a baby," Hein said, standing there on the shoulder of the road. He zipped open the top of his jacket to demonstrate.

The driver raised his eyebrows when he saw the child. He shook his head. "The back or nothing," he said.

By the time the lorry stopped for them, they'd been waiting on the side of the highway for a long time. Before that Hein had had to trudge the stretch of dirt road from the farm. His arms had gone numb from carrying the child and the baggage. This ride was their only option. Hein chucked the rucksack and plastic bags in the back and then carefully clambered up himself, one hand around the boy like a pregnant woman's around her belly.

Once Hein was on board, the driver opened his window and shouted: "You know I'm going to Lesotho, right?"

"That's where we're going as well."

"You're sure?"

Hein nodded, even though he wasn't, and even though the driver couldn't see him. After a few seconds the lorry pulled off.

And here they are now, sitting on a pile of sacks of coal, Hein and the sleeping baby. It's not as hard as he would've expected, the coal, but not exactly comfortable either.

Hein lies down flat on his back, the little boy still on his chest. The moon is travelling along with them up there, a loyal companion. He strokes the child's back. "I'm still thinking, little boy, I'm devising a plan," he says. "I know things are a bit complicated right now, we don't know what the future holds. But I had to rescue you. Those other okes aren't up to looking after you. Not that I really know how either, to be honest, but I'll learn. Just give me a break, let me figure things out . . . " The baby's mouth explores his breast, then he lies still again. Hein smells the long grass lining the sides of the road. Over the months he's developed a fine nose for this dusty perfume. "Do you want to head to Lesotho, baby? For now, I'd say, let's go with the flow. Maybe we can find an abandoned hut in the mountains, or someone can teach me to build one. Then we can live there between clay walls, with dung floors. I can keep cattle for us and grow vegetables. I can wrap a blanket round you and carry you on my back, like the women in the fields. Our skins will get to know each other, every groove and crease . . . "

Talking helps Hein forget the wind and the cold. He places both hands on the bundle on his breast. "Ja, buddy. I'm telling you. We'll find a way. Maybe we should become wanderers on the highways and byways. The sun will warm our heads, the wind will blow at our backs. And the universe will provide. Lorries will pick us up and take us where we need to go. And in the veld animals will graze with us, the donkeys and sheep, all the creatures that you like to touch. The dassies will spy on you from the ridges, the eagles will guard you from way up high." While Hein is holding forth, another truck passes them, howling. The plastic bags around them flutter wildly. The darkness releases black odours, rubber and tar assailing his nostrils. And coal dust.

Hein is talking with his mouth against the child's scalp.

"You need someone to show you the world, kiddo. Someone who can teach you stuff. How to live free, not be tied down. How to find your own compass. How to need nobody, but never to be lonely."

The half-asleep face explores Hein's neck. The small feet trample his thighs. "Fellow travellers, kid, you and me. We'll keep travelling with the light. Faster than the world spins. Darkness won't catch up with us. We don't need a house. In the light, that's where we'll find a home . . . "

The air brakes shudder like a steam train when the lorry stops. The boy starts mewling. Hein sits up. The baby is crying quite a bit now, hiccupping in between. He quietens down, his mouth making a sucking motion, as if there's an invisible teat between his lips. Hein peers over the edge of the truck. There are lights, a fence, a small building. The driver gets out, stretching. He looks up at Hein.

"Time to get off, guy. To show your passports."

"Passports?" Hein doesn't even have one himself. Never mind the kid. Shit, he doesn't even have a birth certificate or anything for him. Maybe he should've looked for it in the cottage. He slaps his temple. What did he think was going to happen, here on the border?

"Can't we just stay up here? You can cover us with sacks. I'll keep the baby quiet."

The driver looks as if he's popping a coronary. He throws up his hands. "Are you crazy? Do I look like a people smuggler to you? And you think they won't check the back of the truck? Where did you find that child anyway? No, wait, I don't want to know. Get lost, man! Down, the both of you!"

"Okay, okay, pal. Chill out." Hein throws the rucksack and baby bags onto the ground, climbs down carefully with the boy. He walks away for some distance, stopping at the edge of the floodlight on the South African side of the border. He stands there for a moment with the crying baby. Further along, a woman is sitting with a sleeping child on her back, tied there with a blanket.

"Why do you look so black?" At first he doesn't get what she means. Then he looks down at his clothes, sees he's covered in coal dust. She looks at the crying child while Hein tries to soothe him. She points upwards. Hein looks up. Dense clouds are billowing over the moon. "That's the thing with little boys," the woman says. "When the sky looks like that, their tummies are not so good." She rubs her own stomach, making a face.

"He's just hungry," Hein says, turning away. The truck has pulled off the road and the border police are getting into the back to check the sacks. Just as well he didn't try to hide there with the baby. Hein walks into the light, to a building where people have formed a short queue. He joins the back of the queue. The child is still crying. An old man who has just reached the front of the queue indicates to Hein that he can go first. Hein performs a thank-you gesture. The policeman behind the counter looks half asleep. "I wanted to ask," Hein says, "if you have hot water for me. To make a bottle for the baby." He has to speak up so that the man can hear him over the child's crying.

The policeman's face doesn't change expression. "Sir, does this look like a hotel to you?"

"No, but—"

The policeman ignores him, signalling to the old man behind him to come forward. Hein walks away, back to where he was. The baby cries more loudly. Hein rubs his head, rocking him. Nothing helps.

"Give him a dummy," says the woman with the blanket around her back, who's still sitting there. Oh, yes, Hein thinks. He rummages in a bag, finds one. The baby quietens down, sucking frantically. Everything is weird on this border, Hein thinks. So unreal. Like in a frozen movie scene.

"I told you," says the woman. "When the clouds look like that, that's when their tummies struggle." Hein rolls his eyes, starts walking away from the border. His arms are aching with the weight of the boy and the bags, and his legs feel the weight of the rucksack. He looks up at the clouds, like massive silent waves, and pushes his hand in between his own belly and the child's. Toasty warm, the heat of togetherness. He walks roughly two hundred metres, then sits down in the dark. A car approaches from the direction of the border. He gets up, lifting his thumb. The car drives past. He sits down again. After about ten minutes there are more lights. A truck this time. The driver stops. At least it's a closed truck. The driver indicates he can get in the back. It turns out, he's not the only one. There are six other men, labourers. Two of them are smoking. They nod at him. When car lights shine on him, they see the baby in his jacket. A couple of the men say something in Sotho. They clear a space for him. He wants to ask them to stop smoking, for the child's sake, but decides to say nothing. They don't look like the friendliest of dudes.

Hein closes the door, the truck pulls off. A bunch of stuff is vibrating back here. Hein's eyes adjust to the dark. The smokers' cigarettes also shed a bit of light. There are pieces of iron, like maybe for construction. Power tools. That kind of thing. It smells of iron and rust. The baby is crying again now. He searches for the dummy, which has fallen, but doesn't find it. Hein regards the vague forms of the other men. A few of them resume talking, shaking their heads. The boy is crying louder and louder now. Hein clutches him closer, the tiny arms folded against his chest. This doesn't silence the little one.

Hein can only see the men's eyes when they draw on their cigarettes, but he senses their hostility. "What?" he says. His voice is more pissed off than he intends. "I can't help it, okay? I have to give the child his milk. But nobody wants to help me. Don't any of you have a thermos or something, with hot water?"

Heads are shaken, tongues click. There's a mumbling, Hein is pointed at. The child also senses something, he's getting hysterical. Hein tries to rock him, but that just makes him bawl even louder. One man knocks on a panel on the side of the cabin. Again and again. Two others join him. They kick up a racket that's louder than the boy's screaming. The brakes are applied. Hein feels the truck pulling off the tar and stopping. The driver comes to open the back, shouting something. The others explain hectically, talking at the same time, pointing at Hein.

"You," the driver says, also pointing at Hein. "Out!"

Hein starts saying something, but one of the others slaps him on the shoulder, pointing at the door. "Come on!" says the driver. "Out!" Hein holds up one hand in surrender, the other on the baby's back. He gathers his stuff, tosses it to the ground, climbs down with the child. The driver gets back into the cabin. The truck drives off.

The rucksack and the bags lie at Hein's feet. The baby senses the silence, or otherwise he's given up. He's gently whimpering now. On the road nothing stirs, there are no lights, near or far. You'd wait forever for a ride here, Hein thinks. For longer than a baby can go without milk. Perhaps they can walk to a garage, where he can find hot water.

He shrugs on the rucksack, picks up the bags, starts walking. He's not sure how far he'll get, but let's see. He talks to the baby, letting the words flow free, where the elements direct. "Don't worry, kid. We're safe. The heavens will protect us. We'll follow the storms. And the moon will light the way."

His arms can't take any more. And there's a long uphill ahead. But he sees something in the moonlight, some distance from the road, a building of some kind. He takes off his rucksack, tosses it over the fence, wriggles through, with the boy, careful that the barbs don't nick him. He walks through the grass, feeling better already, even though his ears are freezing. "The stars will be our guide," he continues. His voice is now the colour of the moon. "The smoke of our fires and the smell of our food will invite kindred spirits from the night . . . "

It's a ruin, he sees when he gets there, an old farmhouse. In the moonlight he can also see a dilapidated kraal. And a trough. He dumps his stuff in the ruin, everything except the baby. He takes out a torch, walks to the trough, shines a light into it. There's some water, but it looks pretty septic. He hears something, walks down the slope. The boy tries to lift his head, wanting to latch on to Hein. There's a narrow stream, with running water. Hein crouches down, dipping his hand in. Freezing. That's all there is. He fills a bottle. By the light of his torch he reads the side of the formula tin, measures out the right amount. He just hopes nothing's been shitting in the water upstream. He holds the bottle of milk in his armpit for a long time, trying to warm it. It doesn't really make a difference. He sits down with his back to the stone wall inside the ruin, zips open his jacket. The baby latches almost violently, as if to devour the teat. When the cold milk hits his throat, he lets go and starts crying. Hein tries again, and again. The boy makes his peace with the cold milk, drinks it.

Silence, at last. The child's stomach is full. For a while, at any rate. And he's asleep on top of Hein. Hein's shoulder is aching where it presses against the wall. He slides down against the rough stone, onto his back, unrolling the sleeping bag and pulling it over them with one hand.

As Hein lies on his back, a name leaps into his mind: Motlale. His head is fuzzy, he can't immediately recall where he heard it. But it feels right. That's what he'll call the child, this baby who has yet to get used to his new father. And now to his new name.

"The sky up there is the colour of the deep ocean," he tells Motlale softly. "There where the monsters swim." Hein stops talking, listens. To twigs rustling with little animals crawling around, birds shaking out their feathers. He sniffs the perfume borne on the night wind.

Hein slows down his breathing, trying to synchronise it with Motlale's. But the child's breath is uneven, like an engine misfiring. Hein can smell himself, a long day's sweat. For the little boy, of that he's sure, this smell is already home.

Motlale groans from time to time. His head moves in his sleep, searching. Hein has no clue what more the baby could need. He pushes his hand in under his jacket, pulls up his shirt, so that the child is lying on his bare skin. The face keeps searching between the few hairs on his chest.

After that first chat on the back of the coal truck, Hein now doesn't really know how to talk to the child. They have yet to find their own language. And that's not going to be invented in one night. "Let's begin at the beginning," he says. "Who are we, kiddo?" Hein touches his own breast. "I'm Hein." Then he taps the boy's chest (gently, gently). "And you are Motlale."

Motlale utters a few tiny sobs, echoes of all the crying earlier. His breath is warm and sweet. Hein feels the child's guts stirring. His own guts could teach the kid's a thing or two. Their stomachs buzz and groan, talking to each other, their juices trading secrets.

It's getting colder and colder. Hein pulls the sleeping bag closer over the child, leaving only his mouth free for breath.

"That's what I can offer you, little one: the sounds of my guts and the beating of my heart. And my skin and my hands and my fingers." Hein stops talking. The moon is now pale and remote. A pine tree protrudes above the walls of the ruin. Perhaps a boy lived here once, Hein thinks, when there was still a roof. And he played under that tree. But it grew too tall, too scary for a child. Sadness descends on Hein like a fog. The baby groans when he presses him close.

"Let me tell you a bit about my family, Motlale." Hein listens to his own voice. It sounds so intimate, enclosed between the stone walls "For starters, there are my mother and my sister in PE. All the doors of their house are locked tonight. Both of them are sleeping without dreams. The dog as well, she doesn't hear a sound. It used to be my dog, you know, long ago. A mongrel bitch with a soft heart, I left her there when I buggered off. There's a prefab concrete wall protecting them all. The sand from the sea blows and blows up against that wall, it'll eventually grind it away . . .

"But now you're interrupting me, little Motlale. What are you saying? You want to know about my *father*? I don't know where he's kipping tonight, or any night for that matter. Maybe in some dry, sandy place. I have zero memory of him. He left when I was three. 'Namibia,' my mother said when I started asking. 'He's an engineer on the diamond mines. He does important work there in the desert. But he's coming back. Then he's bringing us diamonds.' I told her that I was also going to be an engineer one day, so that I could go and work on the same mine. Well, he never came back. And I didn't become an engineer. Didn't go and work in the desert. And no-one brought any diamonds."

Hein zips open his rucksack, slowly and stealthily, taking out a flask of brandy. "See, Motlale," he whispers, "I also have a bottle."

He continues his story. Motlale is still listening, eyes closed. And the ruin and the grasses and the shrinking moon—everything is listening. After he dropped out of his studies, Hein goes on, he went home, back to his mother. For a while he just coasted. Waited, meditated. His sister was also still living at home. She was a year younger than him. At that stage she was just starting at university. But she's a success, done with studying, is an accountant now. They never saw eye to eye, to put it mildly. She always thought Hein was a bit of an idiot. "You're like a child," she kept saying. But there's something else that he can never forgive her for: "Your father," she once declared, "was just as useless as you."

"He's your father too," he replied. "And he's actually an engineer on a mine. A pretty important job. How would you know, anyway? You were hardly born when he left."

She laughed. "You *are* a child. Lapping up all that stuff Mom feeds you. Do you genuinely still believe it? Let me tell you a thing or two. Our father has been wandering in the wilderness for something like twenty years. Stoned and lost. Couldn't keep down a job. Pretty much homeless." At first, his sister continued, he did try to make contact with Hein, but their mother did everything in her power to prevent it. "He didn't show much interest in me," his sister said, her voice changing. "Only in his son."

The next day, before he could confront his mother about his sister's bullshit, his mother told him it was probably time for him to go and live on his own. Find a job, do something with his life. "I scraped and saved and sweated blood to let you study. It didn't work out. And now you're just loafing around." He didn't set a good example for his younger sibling, she said. Somewhere in the passage, Hein knew, his sister was eavesdropping.

"Okay," he said, "why not just say: I'm a fuckup. And I

don't belong in this house. I'll go, I'll go and look for my father." Even though he knew only too well that he had no clue where to start looking. His father had the same name as him. That's all he knew. He's searched on Facebook a thousand times. There are plenty of Hein Vermeulens, but not one that could conceivably be his father.

He went to the bedroom, he tells the baby, where he'd slept as a boy, to start packing. "If they engrave a picture of me on my tombstone, Motlale, it'll have to be of me stuffing gear into a rucksack. Always on the road."

His mother left him alone for a while, then came to his room again. She got all emotional when she saw him packing, started telling him about when he was a baby, how he regularly woke up with his hands frantically reaching upwards, as if he was falling and trying to grab onto something. She asked the paediatrician about it. It's an old instinct, the doctor explained, and the only fear humans are born with. When the baby feels he's falling, the reflex kicks in. As if they're apes, and still swinging around in trees. As if the ape mother had let go of the ape child, and he had to cling on not to fall to the forest floor.

Hein takes another sip of brandy, checks the pulse in Motlale's neck.

When Hein's mother was done, he had something to tell *her*. He'd recently seen a photo, he said, on social media. Of a dead alien found in the veld near PE. A weird, long, thin creature. Turns out, when an expert examined the creature, it was a baby baboon. After he'd died, his mother carried him around for a long time. From being clutched so tightly for so long, his little half-rotten corpse had stretched and dried out till it looked like something from another planet. "I'm sure," he said, looking at his mother, "she only let go of him because the troop intimidated her. Because they were freaked out by the rotten baby. She would never have dropped him of her own accord. And I bet she came to look for him later, but couldn't find him because he'd been carted off by the rubbernecks."

Then his mother started crying bitterly, saying she didn't want him to leave. "Stay, please. Stay."

"I'll stay if you tell me how to contact my father. Where is he?"

She shook her head, her lips clenched together. "I have no idea, Hein. I lost contact with him years ago."

"Well, either you or my sister is lying to me. All I ever wanted was to see him, just once. And I figure if it wasn't for you, I would have."

She started crying again. It was guilty crying, he decided. He waited for her to speak, to blurt it all out, *something* to help him. Waited for her to say no, once would never have been enough for you, you would've wanted to get to know your father, and *that* I couldn't allow. But nothing. Not a word.

Hein cleared out. He left the two women behind in that house on the busy street and never saw them again. The dog, the bitch with her sad ears, stood behind the gate as he walked off. Not a sound, the sand blowing into her eyes.

Hein drains the last sip of brandy. Here he is, lying on his own in the moonlight. With a child—*his* child now—on his breast. Their plans will gradually take shape. Tomorrow they will start walking. If they walk the land for long enough, he and Motlale, they'll get to know all the dusty invisible people on the footpaths; sooner or later, they'll come across his father. Even if it takes years, even if it happens only when Motlale is an older boy with his own pair of strong legs.

Hein looks at the black pine tree above the ruin. "You," he says to Motlale, "I'm going to make something of you.

Something that my mother couldn't make of me. What I would have been had I known my father."

Hein dreams that he's floating in the guts of God. He listens to the noise of the universe, to the holy intestines screaming out secrets. All deep knowledge is imparted to Hein, in a dense stream of revelations. This is what he's been awaiting for so long, what he emptied himself for in the Free State grasslands, what he meditates and suffers and dwells on the edge of precipices for. But now that it's here it's too much, much too much, for one man. His head will shatter.

When Hein half-wakes—it's still night—he thinks at first that the weight on his chest is a stone. Then he feels no, it's a living weight. He opens his eyes properly. The baby's head is up against his lips—that soft spot where you can poke your finger right through into the brain. He doesn't remember the voices in God's guts. He no longer has access to any of the revelations from the noise of the dream. It was like standing in front of a giant speaker at a rock festival and being blown away.

And now he listens. Nothing. God's noise has deafened him. But no, there it is: the sound of a night bird. A little cheep, right here in the ruin. Brave and pure. And, here in his neck, the baby's whimper. Better, he thinks, than God's noisy oracular guts. Motlale's sleepy little hand nestles in Hein's armpit hair. He takes the other hand between his fingers. He thinks of what he once said to Shelley, about hands. Now more than ever, with these tiny, sleepy fingers clutching his own, he knows that hands are made to link people to each other. If everybody could understand this, war and suffering would be obsolete. If everybody could hold hands, humanity would be one long chain of bodies with a single rhythm. Perhaps it's not at the level of the dream's lost knowledge. But for now, with the little boy's sounds, it's enough for him.

He presses his lips to the child's scalp, closing his eyes. If they can lie here like this for long enough, they will grow into each other.

Hein looks up at the bright light. The morning is like cold ash. He feels stiff, and once again is surprised at the child on his chest. Hein licks his finger, places it in front of Motlale's mouth to check that he's breathing. He gets up, puts the baby down on a jersey. He makes a bottle and feeds the boy. He gave him milk once in the dark morning hours as well. And changed his ballooning nappy at last. He cried a lot, little Motlale, lying bare-bummed between the stone walls.

Hein thinks back to how, as a teenager, he used to ask his mother about when he was a baby. She could only remember boring things, like that he was always hungry ("And then you turned out so skinny!"). Or that he was forever bumping his head ("No surprise there," his sister remarked from behind her magazine). Or that he often just lay there gazing into the sky ("Not much has changed," was his sister's comment). Even these few generic scraps of information endeared him to his infant self. Gave him a glimpse of his true nature. Untouched, unspoilt. He wishes he could wipe out the years between. Wishes he could stand in front of baby Hein now, warning him. But he wouldn't know what to say. Whatever crap he came up with would surely just fuck him up all over again, just in different ways. Grown-up Hein can't save baby Hein. Nor his mother. It's his *father* that he needs to hear from. If Hein could ask him just one question, get his attention for one minute, he would know himself for the first time. Would be whole, renewed, his process complete. With everything as it should be.

The child has finished drinking. Hein gently feels the tummy, tight as a drum. Hein lays him down on a blanket, walks off a little way to the rucksack, looks back. There the baby is lying: in a random ruin, close to a random highway. With another steaming nappy. Without the nocturnal brandy, Hein must admit, it doesn't look like the next adventure is around the corner. In front of him is a child who needs to grow up. And somebody needs to care for him. Every day and every night. Somebody needs to keep him warm, give him a soft bed. And playmates, toys, an education, stuff like that. Needs to play with him, teach him things. Somebody who won't fuck him up over and over again. If Hein knows anything, this cold morning, it's that that person, the one who will organise birthday parties for Motlale, buy him a tricycle and swing him on a swing, is not Hein.

Yes, there Motlale lies. And Hein could pick up his rucksack and walk away. He could climb through the fence and wait for a truck to stop. He could, standing there, pretend not to hear anything from the ruin. He'd sit in the wind on the back of the truck and think of nothing. The little boy would live here in this house forever. In the shade of the branches, in the light of the moon, while the night birds sing so bravely. Motlale: the owner of a ruin with a pine tree in its garden. Hein bends, takes the strap of the rucksack in his hand, testing the weight. He straightens again. He can't. Not now that the child has a name.

He sits down on the blanket, taking Motlale on his lap. Offers him the teat again. The baby starts sucking. He doesn't care whether it's Hein feeding him milk or Theon or Daniel or Malefu or a family member or, for that matter, a total stranger. For the time being, at least, it's all the same to him.

Hein is walking down the dirt road leading to the farmhouse and Daniel and Theon's white cottage. He and Motlale have hitchhiked here, this time at least in the cabin of a truck.

A driver who wanted to chat, wanted to hear about the kid. But Hein was done with chatting. Walking, he's got Motlale inside his jacket again, even though it's late morning and the winter sun is nice and toasty. Hein stares like a laser, trying to see what's going on at the cottage ahead. Then he sees it: The sun shines on a white car that isn't Daniel and Theon's bakkie. Also not his own clapped-out Nissan that's been parked there for months. The police? His heart starts thumping. He slips off the dirt road, onto a footpath that he knows. He walks around the back of the poplar grove, through the long grass, past the graveyard, approaching the outside room from behind. Motlale starts crying. Hein hunkers down in the grass. "Shht," he tells the child and covers the little mouth, but that only increases the crying. Hein moves away again, back to the poplars. He skulks, half-crouching, to the trees, the rucksack heavy on top of him, the child heavy under him. The trees hopefully muffle the sound somewhat, but the boy doesn't stop crying.

Hein takes off the rucksack, sits down. He rocks the child in his arms with increasing vigour. "They'll hear you," Hein says. "You must be quiet now. They'll come to fetch us and chuck us in a police van." The baby doesn't heed him, just carries on crying. He rummages in one of the bags. He finds a bottle of medicine, and another one, doesn't really know what they are. Rather something he knows, he thinks. He opens his rucksack and finds a Panado. He scoops a bit of spruit water into a baby bottle, crushes the pill and mixes the powder in. He gives it to the baby, who makes a face, but Hein keeps trying until it's all drunk. Motlale cries louder; he rocks the child frantically. "Shht, little boy, quiet. Please. They'll hear you and come and catch us." Hein waits five minutes, but the child keeps crying. "Enough!" Hein says. "If they hear us, I'll spend the rest of my life in a jail out here in the sticks."

He scratches around, finds a sleeping pill that Shelley gave him once. He breaks it, feeding half to the child. He waits about ten minutes, the child is silent now. He peers through the leaves. He's not sure, it looks as if there's movement around the white car now. Then Motlale starts making a low kind of humming sound, like a tuneless song. Hein keeps listening for footsteps, voices. He whispers fervently: "Come on, dude. I need absolute silence. The light here reflects sound in all directions. Like a huge fucking crystal, scattering light." The child won't stop making a noise. Hein rocks him, holds him tighter. Nothing helps. He scrounges in one of the baby bags, finds a bottle of paracetamol syrup. He holds Motlale in the crook of one arm, supported on a rock, holds the bottle to the child's lips. Hein's elbow slips from the rock, a big blob of syrup oozes into the child's mouth. The baby splutters and chokes, he cries drowsily, gulping. Fuckit, Hein thinks. What have I done now? He wipes the sticky pink medicine from the child's chin and his own arm. He checks the bottle. Shit, there's practically nothing left. He looks down, hoping that some of it landed on the ground.

He waits a while. Motlale's eyes are closed, he is calm. Hein starts loading himself up with the rucksack, the child and the bags. Hein the pack animal. He walks. Passing the graveyard, he recalls Daniel's poem at Malefu's burial, the one about green leaves. Apart from a few poplars there are hardly any trees around here. Just grass and more godforsaken grass. It would've been better to choose a poem that fits this landscape, about waving fields of grass, that kind of shit. Somebody must have written about veld that always looks exactly the same. Even though individual blades die all the time and fresh ones grow up in their place, it's always the same ocean of grassy waves.

The strange car is still parked at the cottage, Hein sees.

There doesn't seem to be any movement now. He's going to leave Motlale in the outside room. They'll find him there. Hein takes the child, who is quiet at last, starts walking through the grass. He approaches the room from the back, opens a window, gently lowers the child to the floor, then the bags with baby stuff. Hein drops the rucksack outside, clambers through the window. He places pillows from the bed in the middle of the floor, laying the child on top. He quickly glances through the front window, towards the cottage. Nothing stirs there. He takes out his notebook, opens it, writes across a double page, in big letters: *MOTLALE*. He places it next to the child.

The baby is uttering faint gurgles. Small bubbles emerge from his mouth, a trickle of pink syrup runs from the corner of his mouth. The eyes try to open, but close again. Gentle, this child. So gentle. So delicate, you can't even see him breathing any more. Hein remains sitting like that with him for a while, holding his hand. He touches the knuckle of each of the limp fingers. One by one. Counting them. He wonders whether the child will wake up, but it's okay. Everything is okay. Here in the grass, where you can float or fall, come or go. Sleep or wake, live or dissolve. Ultimately it's all the same.

He climbs out of the back window, picks up his rucksack. Now he remembers more words from Daniel's poem. The one he quoted next to Malefu's grave. It just pops into his head unbidden: "Begin afresh, afresh, afresh." He could've made a song out of it. Once upon a time. But there's no music left in his head. To be honest, his tunes were never the greatest.

He walks around the back of the poplar grove again. At a meditative pace. He starts missing the weight against his chest, like you'd miss your own lungs, a fierce ache. He walks along the double-track dirt road. He walks on the left, leaving the right free for Motlale, as if he might walk next to him. Hein glances across, half expecting a row of little footprints. But over his shoulder he can see only his own. He looks down at his shoes. The colour of dust. And his sleeves? They look just like the earth and the grass. He's becoming invisible.

He stops by the side of the highway. Stands listening to his own breath, smelling his own sweat. His next mission is to look for his father. And if Hein wants to find him, he must go where the universe leads him. It doesn't matter which side of the road he waits. He'll get in the first truck, in whichever direction.

He raises his arms. They have no weight. He opens his palms, looks at them. Never, he thinks, has anything destroyed a heart like the emptiness of these two hands.

5.
THE CITY OF FATHERS AND SONS

Daniel flares his nostrils at the familiar aroma of dust, the perfume of blond grass. It's early afternoon. Early autumn. The grass stalks feel brittle and dry against his arms as he walks. In all the years of his absence he remembered only silence, but no, he realises now: A light wind perpetually hums in your ears. The soundtrack of the Free State.

He'd planned to drive up to the graveyard, hoping that the farm roads still existed. He's been moving with difficulty of late. His left hip should've been replaced long ago. He just couldn't face having himself reassembled piecemeal with cobalt or chrome or titanium or ceramic—or whatever material ultra-technology nowadays considers appropriate for synthetic joints. No, he'd rather go to pieces gradually. Become a ruin, a piece of flotsam. He has no interest in preserving himself. Becoming a kind of collage, an artefact in mixed media. Not that he particularly hankers after oblivion, or wants to claim martyrdom. Old age, after all, befalls most living creatures. He wants to allow a natural progression, will see the dissolution through calmly. (Calmly? he thinks. Ha! Just wait until the torment becomes worse, much worse, than a troublesome hip.)

The car had to be left next to the main road, at the gate to the twolane track, where he'd got out to try the chain and lock. He hadn't foreseen that the gate might be locked. He could have got back into the car and charged through the gate at speed. The chain was flimsy and rusted, would have yielded easily. But his ever more retiring northern-hemisphere self didn't feel up to the procedures generated by damage to a rental car. He climbed through the fence, or what remained of it, with some effort, is now proceeding step by step along the dirt road. His frame aches; his balance is unreliable. He refuses to use a support—a crutch or stick or, god help us, some kind of steel frame to trundle ahead of you. As long as he can stay upright, he'll do his own walking, thank you. It's not been travelled for a long time, this road. The grass in the central ridge is as tall as on the verges. He's grateful that his doddering is hidden from sight under the grass line. Not that there's anyone around to see.

He stops some distance from the farmhouse. It's obviously uninhabited. Windows and doors have been removed, sections of the corrugated-iron roof are gone. Looking to the left, he can see the cottage showing above the grass some distance away. Its roof has also been stripped. He is a (laboriously) walking cliché, he thinks. The South African returning to wreckage in a sea of grass. Here on the old farm. He wanted to escape the wrecks, but time and again has found himself back among them. At least no long-lost family members await him, there's no bone-weary old dog wagging its tail. And there is nothing baroque or romantic about the remains of the building. They are vandalised structures rather than crumbling ruins. The windows and doors, one can only hope, are now being put to use somewhere else, built into more hospitable dwellings. Where the inhabitants take comfort from living at peace with other people. Where you can hear your neighbour sigh and toss and turn at night, behind tin walls. Where people look after each other's children, eat together, perhaps share their bodies more readily, and, who knows, steal each other's possessions. How typical of his ancestors, by contrast, to come and isolate themselves like this. To impose property rights on grass, for miles and miles around, and to end their days in a vacuum. In bleak structures like these. Like surly orphans in the midst of the boundless undulation.

Now only the barren walls survive in the pallid light. An abstraction, more or less. And yet, approaching the house, he sees that it squats in the centre of a vegetable garden. Pumpkin plants thrive everywhere, fresh and abundant. There is life here after all! Children close by, perhaps, who will grow pot-bellied on the sweet golden pulp. It lightens his mood. Even gladdens him. The abstraction is suspended.

He walks closer, collapses among the leaves, sits down flat on the warm ground. He cautiously fingers a leaf, bends and sniffs at a pumpkin. After a while he tries to get to his feet, but sinks back into the loam. He shouldn't have sat down, he realises. His hip has locked, like a machine part seizing. He grabs at the hairy stalks, trying to pull himself up by them. A futile effort. They crush in his palms, give way. He falls back on one elbow. Now he's leaning back at an angle among pumpkin tendrils, useless as a rusty plough. He rolls over, hoping that he's not twining himself into the spiralling vines of the pumpkin plants. Now he's on all fours. He hangs his head, catching his breath. He watches in surprise as a thimbleful of moisture appears under him, as if welling up from underground. He moves a hand, dips a finger in it. A trickle of spit, he realises, dribbling from his own mouth and gathering there. He smiles, shaking his head. It could've been worse. Rather a drooling old man than one with a leaking bladder. Although that no doubt also awaits. He stays like that for a while, then supports himself with one hand on a pumpkin, lifting a knee. With a painful effort he struggles to his feet. Beneath his feet is solid ground. He waits for a moment, checking his balance. He looks down at his dirty palms, his dusty knees. Then he surveys the abundance, wondering whether anybody will harvest these pumpkins. He's been taking it for a vegetable garden, but realises now that it's overgrown, unkempt. A no-man's-garden, a deviant relic of a vegetable garden. A predatory pumpkin patch has devoured the other vegetables, colonised the yard. It is starting to twine in through doors and windows, will in time choke and flatten the ruin.

He dusts his hands, walking in the direction of the cottage. His hip is throbbing now. The cottage, he notes when he gets there, has at some point been used as a pen for animals. The front doorway is blocked to hip height with a steel grid. Inside there are mounds of powdery dung: sheep or goats. A crude shepherd's hook leans against the inside wall. Daniel reaches for it over the wire grid. For a moment his balance teeters uncertainly and it feels as if he's going to collapse face first into the dung. He steadies himself, comes upright.

He leans on the stick, testing it, turns round. Something on the horizon has changed. The outside room, he realises. There is no sign of it. Evidently demolished. He turns again, leaning more heavily on his stick, looking back at the farmhouse and yard. Near and far, familiar and unfamiliar. There's no end to his rituals of arrival and departure, he thinks. His life is a thing of false starts and false endings. Rife with truncated adventures, with new chapters after what seemed to be the end of the story. Around him, everybody fades and falls away. But *he* persists. Oh, and of course his sister. A survivor, if ever there was one. Somewhere in London, he's not even sure where, she's leading an elegant though surely lonely widowed existence, her children and grandchildren scattered over North America, Australia and who knows where. He hasn't had a conversation with her in many years. It's painful:

the fact that he still feels the need to contact her, even though he knows in his marrow that the wind would be knocked out of him the moment he heard her voice.

The stick is in his hand. His doddering is now more precarious, after the involuntary stopover in the pumpkin patch. He is even more grateful now that there's nobody here to observe him. Stooped, stick in one hand, the other hand on his hip: a vagabond in an opera.

He's almost there. Here it looms before him: the graveyard. Or what's left of it. Sprawling like a miniature city, though with a new silhouette. Almost all the older stones have collapsed. Or been kicked over perhaps. If it's a city, it's been half destroyed. A city where an aeroplane crashed, or a massive wave washed through. Only in one corner do clustered stones still stand like buildings. He recognises all those that are still upright. He or Theon oversaw the erection of each of them. There is Malefu's skyscraper, its height proportionate to his cousin's feelings of guilt at the time. There is Motlale no.1's modest monument. More than a quarter of a century old, the veins in the marble faded. Then Motlale no.2's, also marble, identical though smaller. Still surprisingly bright after more than a decade, as if illuminated from within. He regards the fourth stone from the corner of his eye. Medium height, sombre grey granite. Like a run-of-the-mill office block. Anonymous, unengraved. Daniel tries, in vain, to ward off memories of his and Theon's last months here on the farm. He can now see the Unnameable One before him: the random visitant, the youthful wanderer. The young man who insinuated himself here, who penetrated his and Theon's lives and then caused them such unasked-for and immeasurable pain.

Initially, he and Theon, he recalls reluctantly, were well-disposed towards him. He could have been their son. And he seemed such a forlorn young soul, especially after his lightweight girlfriend buggered off. What a fateful error it was to take him in, this gangling backroom lodger; what an impossible price was paid.

A few days after he'd disappeared with the child, he was found. Not far from the farm, next to the main road, where he'd been struck by some heavy vehicle and flung into the tall grass. According to the autopsy, he'd lain there for hours before he died. And he'd been dead for quite some time before he was found. Only three days later, when dogs from neighbouring farms started circling the outside room, did Daniel and Theon make the unthinkable discovery . . .

Why had they buried the young man on the farm? Few things mattered any more then. They actually didn't want to get involved, were in any case on the point of finally leaving the farm. But there was a body that had to be dealt with. The young man's family was informed; there were contact details in his rucksack, torn open by the violence of the vehicle, or perhaps by animals, its contents strewn round his lifeless body. When the police informed his mother of the circumstances, of what had happened before his death, she stayed away, didn't want anything to do with her son's body. Daniel and Theon hardly had a choice.

They used the same undertakers as for the baby's burial. If he's become expert at one thing in his life, Daniel thinks, it's arranging funerals. Getting rid of bodies. Nobody apart from the undertakers attended the burial. The two cousins stayed in the cottage, blinds drawn. They did not deliberately leave the stone unengraved like that. It simply got forgotten in the upheaval of arrangements. Or that's what Daniel tells himself. That's how he prefers to remember it. If he were to think back carefully, he knows, he'd remember Theon's vehemence, his relentless resistance. Not to the young man's burial, but to the incision of letters in the stone. To a name memorialised. On the baby's small marble headstone, on the other hand, the name was carved with the greatest care and with the finest chisel. Perhaps, Daniel thinks, he must take a deep breath, and now, while he's here, see to it that the grey stone is finally engraved. In spite of himself, and despite his piety towards Theon. He could extend his stay, postpone his return flight to London. Isn't it his duty to suspend the young man's anonymity? Even though somebody will probably come and topple the stone, or haul it away to build something? Of all the people on earth, only Daniel could do it; he alone would be able to dictate what should be engraved on the granite. When he dies, the young man's name will disappear into nothingness. But he doesn't know. Doesn't know if he's up to it.

His cousin didn't really survive the events. Theon lived on for almost a year, yes, but he was no longer alive. They hadn't been in England for long before Theon was once again diagnosed with cancer. After all those years it had caught up with him again.

After the diagnosis, Daniel started cooking frantically. He drove around to find the best ingredients at local farmers' markets. Deep-red cuts of beef and lamb. Vegetables fresh from the soil, clods still clinging to them. The dim kitchen acquired a glow as he started cooking old-fashioned recipes, one after the other. Stews and soups, pies and steamed puddings. And bread, baked in the Aga.

But Theon rarely ate, and then only potatoes and water. Sometimes an egg, sometimes a bit of rice. Occasionally a slice of buttered bread. Entire meals ended up in the bin.

Daniel had hoped he could do something else for Theon— show him the world, or at least, given his state of health, a few cherished niches within the wider world. Really just the darkly shimmering, velvety relics of a vanished kind of continental existence. He wanted to ease the last months for Theon, erect a shield against the imminent. Daniel made plans, worked out destinations and routes and accommodations: cosy hotels on the Amalfi coast, a voyage on a nineteenth-century Alpine train with compartments of varnished wood, an old-fashioned yacht with blindingly white sails among sun-baked Mediterranean islands. Also the new Europe: a modernist shelter on a windswept Norwegian island, an eco-hut on a Slovenian lake, a minimalist Swiss chalet. He selected places with care, places where Theon would be comfortable, even when he wasn't feeling well. Where they could look out from wide windows onto inhospitable landscapes: granite mountains or wastes of icy water, fierce snowstorms. Or where they could sink away in soft furnishings above a shimmering sea. The gentle light of hotel interiors, the clink of silver cutlery on porcelain, the fume of mature brandy warmed over a candle; things like that would surround them. Just the two of them, sheltered from the elements. Cushioned from the past, free at last.

But Theon's need—indeed his sole remaining urge—was to wander in the Kent countryside. Well, reflects Daniel, "wander," with its associations of leisureliness, of lingering at viewpoints and dallying in the heather, is definitely the wrong word. It was winter. In a waxed raincoat and rubber boots, Theon wanted to contend with the wind. Wordless past cattle and hedgerows. Unseeing past tearooms with lace curtains, past pubs and little stone churches. As if he could stride out of the rain, out of the gruel of mist and mud and low grey skies. Beyond the hunkering cottages and the grass-green meadows, the cobblestones and stone walls, antique shops and market squares. As if he could find a doorway to forgetfulness. And the latter could only be a limitless expanse of blond grass. Theon usually wanted to be on his own in the wind, but Daniel went along when his cousin tolerated it. When they got home, Daniel made a fire in the hearth with frozen fingers, grateful that they could escape the elements. He dried their socks, prepared food. Theon kept pacing the rooms of the house. Endlessly circling. Barefoot, not eating or seeking out the heat of the fire or allowing Daniel to dry his hair. He seemed intent on bringing the violence of the elements into the house with him. It looked as if he wanted to burst through the eighteenth-century walls, or bash his head to a bloody pulp against them. This carried on till he got too ill to walk, lay down on his bed and died a week later amidst unrelenting rain.

This morning, Daniel had driven straight from the airport to Eenzaamheid, or whatever these fields of grass with their ruins are called nowadays. He is surprised at the name's recurrence to him now, at its sudden materialising from thin air. Since his arrival he has not thought of it once. The nameplate has been missing from the gate for decades. He must surely be the last person on earth to associate this land with that name. And how quaint is his bourgeois assumption that it still *has* a name, that the very idea of naming such a place, now vaguely delimited and lacking an obvious owner, would still have any purchase. In any case, he'll have to make his way back quite soon if he wants to catch his late-night flight. Even though he knew such a to-and-fro journey would be exhausting, he hadn't wanted to overnight in South Africa. All he'd wanted was to spend a last few hours here, while he was still capable of movement.

On his way from the airport, it hadn't occurred to him to buy flowers. A flower, in any case, was not a commodity on sale in any of the small towns he passed through. He stopped next to the highway, at a roadside stop with a concrete table and benches, and picked some of the season's last cosmos flowers, a generous bunch. Once there would have been a few paltry pepper trees here, but now there was nothing to screen the sun. The concrete benches were dilapidated, decades old, relics of another era. Daniel stood there by the table, which was half eroded by rain, his arms full of flowers. He shook his head at such a picnic spot, in the eddying of tar fumes and exhaust gases from archaic petrol cars. It must have been bleak, this spot, even when it was new. Can it possibly date from the eighties? Does it embody a planner's fantasy of a little white family unloading their picnic basket from their station wagon, of rosy-cheeked children teasing hard-boiled eggs from tinfoil with delicate fingers? You could think of the table as a tomb, Daniel thought, as the place where such fantasies had found their final resting place. He laid a sheaf of the cosmos flowers on the concrete.

He now realises he's left the remaining flowers in the car when he climbed through the farm gate. He couldn't have walked very far with them in any event, given his lack of balance. They're wilting on the back seat now. If he had them in his arms, he wouldn't mete out stems scrupulously between graves. He would cast them abundantly, strew them like a potentate to a multitude. He looks around him to where the flowers would have fallen. Somewhere in the jumble there are shards engraved with letters that, if assembled like a jigsaw puzzle, would spell out Theon's father's name. Daniel had, shortly after moving in with Theon in the cottage, also come here to cement his own father's urn on top of Theon's father's grave. The shards of the urn are now lying interred in the rubble of the city. The ashes must have drifted off in the wind, are now dispersed, clinging glistening to distant blades of grass.

Thus he and his cousin had gathered their dead, the welcome as well as the unwelcome. Gradually the little populace grew, became complete. Or so they had assumed. Then Theon himself was added to the assembly. Daniel thinks back to the manoeuvres it took to bring his cousin home. He'd had the body transported from Kent to Heathrow and then flown out. Then he'd travelled here himself, and waited for Theon along with the new inhabitants of the farm. There were a good dozen of them in the house, and they were not talkative. Or at least not fluent in English. Daniel had no idea whether these were descendants of Malefu or simply squatters. They tolerated Daniel's presence mildly, displaying no signs of proprietary entitlement, even though they had no clue what he'd come here to do. The farm was simply a place where they were living and eating for the time being, and where Daniel, if he should so wish, could also come to live and eat. That was how he interpreted his reception. In truth, he had no idea what they thought of this presumptuous intruder. Or how they saw their own presence here, or their future, or their relation to the land. Be that as it may, along with Daniel they formed a taciturn reception committee for his cousin.

Conveying the corpse to the farm had proved a logistical nightmare. The specialist movers explained that they were only allowed to deliver cadavers to the care of official mortuaries. And no funeral director was prepared to come out here for the interment. Recent regulations, they informed Daniel, required special permission for the burial of a body outside a municipal cemetery. Daniel had not thought such bureaucratic detail was still being observed here. He no longer had a sense of how things were done in the country, he realised. He had to improvise, do as he thought people went about doing things here. He checked into the town hotel for a week, no longer the Imperial, now the Radiance Tavern Inn. He patiently teased out where unofficial payments were to be channelled to ensure that the body reached the farm. A few days later it was at last delivered. In an anonymous refrigerated van, and in darkness. As if to dump the body of a murder victim. The body was wrapped in a tarpaulin, a rope wound round it. The farm inhabitants watched in silence. Daniel offered some of the young men in the house an exorbitant sum to dig a hole the following morning, next to the marble tombstones; the van driver translated into Sotho for Daniel. The corpse overnighted in the yard of the farmhouse. Daniel slept in his car, or, more precisely, sat half-frozen all night in the driver's seat, a wake of sorts, gazing at Theon's shape lying outside on the hard ground. A lonely bundle.

    The grave was dug at daybreak. The cold soil was unforgiving. The helpers carried Theon down the footpath, feet first. At the graveside they waited for Daniel's sign. When he nodded, they started edging his cousin slowly over the opening. The half-rigid corpse balanced hesitantly on the friable edge for a few moments. Then gravity asserted itself, toppling the body and uncoremoniously sucking it down to hit the bottom with a dull thud. Daniel went to look over the edge, though he shouldn't have. Down there Theon lay in his canvas bag, his posture painfully familiar. On his side, his knees drawn in. Like a hostage.

    Daniel wanted to have a marble headstone erected, similar to those of the two children. None of the undertakers wanted to provide a stone for the illicit grave, and when Daniel tried to contact the marble suppliers himself, it transpired that they no longer existed. He paid his helpers a further sum, and persuaded them with explanatory gestures to roll a hunk of sandstone to this place. Daniel found a local amateur stonemason, a man from Lesotho, who with passable exactitude chiselled a single Christian name on it. With his grey hair he sat here, chipping away. His glasses had the thickest lenses Daniel had ever seen. When the stoneworker regarded his work at a certain angle, the lenses scattered sunlight in various colours all over the stone.

Now Daniel is standing here where the half-blind mason once stood. His hand is resting on the very stone, the letters legible to the palm of his hand. One might think that there's comfort to be found in touching the sun-warm stone like that. But Daniel is doing so in order to stay upright.

He takes a step away from the graves, then retreats further. He stands there, leaning on the stick. His staff, his shepherd's crook, his salvation. Here he is, in the cooling air outside the city. He is not an inhabitant, or even a visitor. Nor even an exile. Actually, his bent and bowed self looks more like a structure of some kind. A weatherworn pier, a useless old crane. A dilapidated factory, a worked-out mine. A piece of machinery, of iron or concrete. Like something in an industrial area or harbour, or on a deserted beach. Nothing that can still be of use to the city.

He turns round, pivoting on the stick. He shields his eyes with his hand, looking for the poplar grove. It's still there. Denser now, and darker. The distance to the trees seems insurmountable. He nevertheless starts walking towards it. As long as he just places one foot in front of the other, he must get there. Then, without any warning, his hip gives in. Or his knee, or foot. Whatever it is, he sinks down into the grass. He sits down. Hard, without control. He grimaces, eyes closed, thinks away the pain. For a while he does not move. Then he lies back. The switches of grass yield gracefully, making room for him. Above him there is nothing, apart from the unbroken blue that spans this southern sky. He lies listening for guineafowl. Nothing. The eleven letters of *E-e-n-z-a-a-m-h-e-i-d* unexpectedly float past in the sky, like smoke signals. He gazes intently at each letter, trying to persuade himself that they are really there. They unravel into wisps, dissolving against the blue.

He closes his eyes, hoping that he won't have to get up again. Stalks of grass offer no more support than a cloud. No, he'll remain floating like this. In this sea of grass that will surge out further and further, until it flows into all the oceans of the earth. Until the undulations start heaving beneath him, lifting him and letting him down, lifting and letting go. Slowly he will move away from the island city of graves, the only bit of solid ground, now, in a thousand sea miles.

Soon enough the shadows of towering ships will fall over him. He will not expect a lifeboat to be lowered to him. Nobody can see him down here. When they have sailed past and grown smaller in the distance, he will feel the sun on his face, the prickling of salt water on his skin, the nibbling of anxious little silver fish.

His bones will become supple like kelp, will bend and sway with the currents. The stick on which he's been leaning will float away, the kilogrammes he weighed just moments ago become impossible to calibrate.

The cure of weightlessness is starting to take effect: Miraculously, he no longer feels his hip. So, like this, he will keep drifting in the translucent sea. Without pain or desire. Until he too becomes water.

About the Author

S.J. Naudé is the author of two collections of short stories, *The Alphabet of Birds* and *Mad Honey*, and two novels, *The Third Reel* and *Fathers and Fugitives*. He is the winner of the Nadine Gordimer Short Story Award, the University of Johannesburg Prize, the kykNet-*Rapport* prize and is the only writer to win The Hertzog Prize twice consecutively in its 100 year history. *The Third Reel* was shortlisted for the *Sunday Times* prize. His work has been published in *Granta* and other journals in the US, UK, Netherlands and Italy.

Europa Editions UK

Read the World

Literary fiction, popular fiction, narrative non-fiction,
travel, memoir, world noir

Building bridges between cultures with the finest writing from around the world.

Ahmet Altan, Peter Cameron, Andrea Camilleri, Catherine Chidgey, Sandrine Collette, Christelle Dabos, Donatella Di Pietrantonio, Négar Djavadi, Deborah Eisenberg, Elena Ferrante, Lillian Fishman, Anna Gavalda, Saleem Haddad, James Hannaham, Jean-Claude Izzo, Maki Kashimada, Nicola Lagioia, Alexandra Lapierre, Grant Morrison, Ondjaki, Valérie Perrin, Christopher Prendergast, Eric-Emmanuel Schmitt, Domenico Starnone, Esther Yi, Charles Yu

Acts of Service, *Didn't Nobody Give a Shit What Happened to Carlotta*, *Ferocity*, *Fifteen Wild Decembers*, *Fresh Water for Flowers*, *Lambda*, *Love in the Days of Rebellion*, *My Brilliant Friend*, *Remote Sympathy*, *Sleeping Among Sheep Under a Starry Sky*, *Total Chaos*, *Transparent City*, *What Happens at Night*, *A Winter's Promise*

Europa Editions was founded by Sandro Ferri and Sandra Ozzola, the owners of the Rome-based publishing house Edizioni E/O.

Europa Editions UK is an independent trade publisher based in London.

www.europaeditions.co.uk

Follow us at . . .
Twitter: @EuropaEdUK
Instagram: @EuropaEditionsUK
TikTok: @EuropaEditionsUK